"HAVE YOU COME TO ANY CONCLUSIONS about me?" Katherine asked.

"You mean, other than you might be crazy?" Peter asked, grinning.

She nodded, and he went on. "No conclusions yet, but maybe some understanding about why you feel the way you do about things." He paused. "Now let's order take-out I'm starving."

"Sure, if you want to, but I cooked," she said, tempting him. "I was so mad at you before, I was going to sit and eat it in front of you. But now I guess I might be persuaded to share it with you."

"What do I have to do to persuade you?" he asked.

"Oh, I'm sure you can think of something," she murmured.

"Let's see. I could run faster than a speeding bullet for you."

"Too tiring."

"Swim an ocean for you?"

"Too long."

"Sit on a flagpole for you?"

"Too painful."

"Wrestle an alligator for you?"

"Too stupid."

"Jump a tall building for you."

"I'd rather you jumped me."

"No problem . . ."

WHAT ARE *LOVESWEPT* ROMANCES?

They are stories of true romance and touching emotion. We believe those two very important ingredients are constants in our highly sensual and very believable stories in the LOVESWEPT line. Our goal is to give you, the reader, stories of consistently high quality that may sometimes make you laugh, sometimes make you cry, but are always fresh and creative and contain many delightful surprises within their pages.

Most romance fans read an enormous number of books. Those they truly love, they keep. Others may be traded with friends and soon forgotten. We hope that each LOVESWEPT romance will be a treasure—a "keeper." We will always try to publish

LOVE STORIES YOU'LL NEVER FORGET
BY AUTHORS YOU'LL ALWAYS REMEMBER

The Editors

Loveswept ® 686

THE ONE FOR ME

MARY KAY McCOMAS

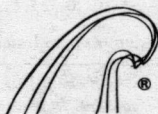

BANTAM BOOKS

NEW YORK · TORONTO · LONDON · SYDNEY · AUCKLAND

THE ONE FOR ME
A Bantam Book / May 1994

*If you would be interested in receiving protective vinyl covers for your
Loveswept books, please write to this address for information:*

Loveswept
Bantam Books
P.O. Box 985
Hicksville, NY 11802

ISBN 0-553-44212-0

Published simultaneously in the United States and Canada

*Bantam Books are published by Bantam Books, a division of Bantam Dou-
bleday Dell Publishing Group, Inc. Its trademark, consisting of the words
"Bantam Books" and the portrayal of a rooster, is Registered in U.S. Patent
and Trademark Office and in other countries. Marca Registrada. Bantam
Books, 1540 Broadway, New York, New York 10036.*

PRINTED IN THE UNITED STATES OF AMERICA

OPM   0 9 8 7 6 5 4 3 2 1

Hello, Dolly!
This one's for you.
I love you.

ONE

Three was their lucky number.

When Katherine and her sisters were young, everything came in threes. Three dresses. Three apples. Three coloring books. You took one and gave one to each of your sisters. They were expected to share. That's the way it was.

They shared the family television. They shared the upstairs bath. A lone, used automobile did triple duty during their high school years. And there was only one face—which was, perhaps, the most annoying of all the shared items.

As they grew older, they didn't share everything. They didn't share their clothes, as their tastes ran in opposite directions. They didn't share a personality; they were as different as day and night . . . well, dusk, dawn, and high noon, let's say. And they never ever shared their men. . . .

"I can't believe we let her do this to us again," Katherine said, shimmying into a too-tight black sheath dress that was cut too low on top and too high at the hem. "Why couldn't we have worn our own clothes? She dresses like a ten-cent hooker."

"She does not. That's a beautiful dress," Quinlyn said, pulling Katherine's angora sweater down over her head and tucking it into tailored slacks. "I felt positively sexy in it. I kept wishing Robert were here."

"I wish he were here too. He never would have agreed to let you do this, and then I wouldn't have had to," she said, stepping into three-inch heels and picking up a brush to rearrange her dark, shoulder-length hair. "You let her get away with murder, Quinn. And then I always end up cleaning up the mess. Why is that? It's time for her to grow up and take some responsibility. She can't keep getting herself into these messes and expect us to get her out of them all the time."

"All the time? She hasn't asked us to do this for her in years." Not too reluctantly she admitted, "Actually, I'm having a great time."

Katherine sent her a look that would have freeze-dried a peach.

"Corrie would do this for you," Quinn reminded her patiently, trying the guilt approach, which always worked so well with Katherine.

"Oh, right. She'd love this. It's stupid, immature, and wrong. Right up her alley." She turned from the rest room mirror to study the part in her sister's hair, then she set about matching it. "The thing is, I'd never arrange two dates with two different men on the same night and ask her to fill in for me. She's unorganized, rude, and totally irresponsible."

"We can't all be perfect."

She rolled her bright blue eyes in her sister's direction.

"I'm not perfect and you know it. But I can keep an appointment, my checks don't bounce, and I can remember to put gas in my car." She pulled her hair away from her face on the right side. "I need the barrette."

Quinn removed the silver barrette from her hair and handed it to Katherine. "Give it up, Katherine. Accept it. You're the wired, uptight one. Corrie's the flake. And I'm the easygoing, normal, and incredibly beautiful triplet. It's been that way for thirty-two years, and I suspect it always will be."

Quinn also had the best sense of humor of the three. The chief ruffled-feather smoother, she was happily married, and the mother of three.

"You're also a pain," Katherine said, grinning at her. "And we'll be thirty-six next fall." She picked up a gold pin shaped like a cow with freshwater pearl teats and pinned it to the dress. It was . . . *udderly* suggestive. "Tell me about the guy. Is he really as dull as wet cardboard?"

"Actually, I've been wondering about that. Corrie must have met him at a bad time. He's not like she described him. He's very good-looking, like she said, but he isn't all business and he isn't at all bossy. He's completely charming and there's . . . I don't know, this energy about him. He's really very . . . well, I have my Robert, of course, but there's something very attractive about this man. I like him."

"Does he speak in complete sentences?"

"Yes. He's an architect. Seems very bright."

"There's the hitch. Corrie likes the stupid ones she can wrap around her finger."

"Joey wasn't stupid."

"That's why they're divorced."

"Katherine. Shame on you. She's your sister."

"You don't need to keep reminding me," she said, taking a final glance between the two of them in the mirror. She looked exactly like the Quinlyn/Corene who'd excused herself from John Wesley's table minutes earlier to visit the powder room. Quinn now looked like the Katherine who'd been waiting for her there. "If this man is so charming, why don't you let me go pick up the kids while you stay and finish dinner?"

"I would, but I told you before, Trevor's going through that separation phase, and I hate leaving him anywhere for too long a time. I trust Molly completely and she always has him settled down by the time I get back, but the whole time I'm gone I feel as if he's thinking I've abandoned him." She shrugged. "It's a crazy mother thing, I know, but I can't help it. And an hour and a half is about all I can take. You'll have to finish the dinner. Besides, if we take the time to change clothes again, he'll think Corrie's constipated or something."

"Why do I find that a temptation?"

"Because you'd like everyone to think you're a poop instead of the good, caring soul you are. Now hurry up and get back out there. We were talking about the River Vista Project when I left."

"I thought you said he wasn't all business? What do I know about the River Vista Project?"

"As much as I know, which is what Corrie told us. Just look interested and ask him a lot of questions. It's just this one night, and it's an important account for her."

"Then she ought to be here."

"And she would be," Quinn said calmly, pushing Katherine toward the door. "But her relationship with Michael is a little unsteady right now, and going to his business dinner with him is a little more important, don't you think?"

"What would she do if she didn't have two look-alikes to fill in for her? What would any other woman, including you and me, do in this situation?"

"Seems to me, you've asked me that question before. About a hundred times. And I still don't know the answer. I'm not Corrie."

"Well, I'm not either, and look at me. Lord, I hate the way she dresses, and I don't want to talk about some river renovation project I know nothing about with some man I've never met before. I really hate this."

"I know," she said sympathetically, holding the door open for her. "And next time, I'll stand firm. I promise. I won't back down, no matter what sort of mess she's gotten herself into. She'll have to take care of it on her own."

"I want that in writing."

"Lord above, you legal types are all alike. Get going," she said, giving her sister a little shove. "And smile. Look friendly. Enjoy your dessert."

"Dessert? You ate all the food?" She looked dejected beyond description. "I'm starving."

"So was I."

Katherine watched Quinn scurry around the partition toward the exit before she forced herself to turn in the opposite direction.

"Pssst. Katherine." Quinn was back.

"What," she whispered.

"*I'm* thirty-two."

Katherine walked across the elegant French restaurant to the cozy booth her sister had directed her to earlier.

God knew, she more than loved her sisters, but would a face of her own have been asking for too much? she wondered.

She was fully aware of the male gazes that followed her as she passed table after table. And where Corrie might enjoy having her cleavage ogled and her legs gawked at, Katherine found it demeaning and thoroughly embarrassing, and couldn't wait to be seated safely behind a table. She stepped up her pace, then had to slow down a bit for fear of falling off Corrie's ridiculously high heels.

Then, like a messenger from a kind god, a waiter appeared out of nowhere. He stepped forward and pulled the table out, allowing her to slip straight into the booth without having to stand on display as she waited.

Unconsciously, she released a marathon runner's sigh.

"Well, that didn't take too long," John Wesley said, smiling.

She glanced at him, ready to simper and bat her eyes in the usual Corrie fashion. Instead, she felt her mouth fall open and her eyes grow wide. Her stomach did a backflip. Fireworks exploded in her head. Her heart jumped into her throat. Was she breathing? Yes. Yes, she was, but a little too fast. She felt dizzy.

"What is it?" he asked, concerned. "Are you all right?"

"Yes. Yes, of course," she said, her breath gaspy. Dear Lord of the earth and the moon and the stars and the heavens above! He was gorgeous! "I . . . I must have sat down too quickly. I . . . I'm fine. Really. I'm okay."

"Are you sure? You look flushed."

She giggled, though she hadn't meant to. Giggling was so . . . so . . . Corrie. And Corrie was the last person she wanted to think of just then.

"Lower altitude," she said, words spilling from her mouth from an unknown and obviously unbalanced source. "These heels are too high."

He chuckled, but still looked anxious for her.

"Maybe we should check into the nearest hyperbaric chamber. Anton'll slit his wrists if you get the bends in his restaurant."

"No, no. We can't have that. I'm fine. Really," she said, dragging her gaze from his exquisite features to take a sip of water. Breaking contact with the deep dark intensity of his eyes was like getting a boost of air from an oxygen tank. She could breathe again.

"Seriously, if you need some air, we can leave," he said kindly.

"No. I'll eat something and feel better in no time. Really."

"Dessert, then," he said. He was astonished, but hid it well as he politely summoned the waiter to their table. She'd already eaten enough to keep the members of a French lumber camp from starving for a week.

"Dessert for the lady, please," he said, addressing the waiter as if the man hadn't noticed his companion had ordered twice the number of side orders usually considered adequate for a meal at Anton's, then proceeded to wolf the meal down.

The server glanced from Katherine to John, masking his thoughts with long practice. "Can I get you anything else, sir?"

"No, thank you, I'm fine with this," he said, tipping the half-full glass of wine in his hand.

"Very good." He turned and with a flick of his wrist had the dessert cart delivered to him by an underling. "What is your desire, Ms. Asher?"

Ms. Asher? She'd forgotten it was Corrie's favorite restaurant, and that she was well-known there.

"Mmm . . . is that *crème brulée*?" she asked, inspecting the selection with care.

"Yes, miss."

"And what's this?"

"*Riz à l'impératrice*, miss."

"Rice?"

"Yes, miss."

"And this one?"

"*Boules sur chocolat*, miss. Your favorite."

"Hmm . . ." Her stomach was pinched tight and rubbed raw with hunger. She was sure that if she put something filling in it, she could look at John Wesley without sending her innards into orbit again. It all looked so good, but . . .

Well, hell, they all thought she was Corrie anyway!

"I'll take all three, please," she said, smiling innocently at the startled waiter. She waited for the laughter at the back of her throat to subside before she looked at John and said, "I have a little sweet tooth."

It was more like a fang, he suspected, but Corene Asher was a willowy knockout who elevated eating to an art form. She could wrap her lips around a fork full of food like nothing he'd ever seen before. Slow. Sensuous. Erotic. What she'd do with a spoon and something soft had him shifting his weight with anticipation.

"I like women with healthy appetites," he said, wondering if all her appetites were equally as robust.

Katherine caught the play on words but didn't look up. She swallowed hard and picked up a silver spoon.

She started with the thick cream and rice first, taking small bites off the tip of her spoon, licking the bottom with her tongue, indulgently caressing the top with her upper lip.

John bit gently on the rim of his wineglass. He cleared his throat and tried to cross his legs under the table. Her next bite had him vowing to sample the texture and consistency of those lips, the flavor and composition of that tongue, sometime very soon. Hopefully, before the night was over.

"So, tell me what you have in mind for our campaign," he said, leaning back, stretching his arm across the back of the seat behind her. "We're going to need plenty of good press on this one."

"I'm still thinking," she said per Corrie's directive, not quite able to look him in the eye yet. "Tell me more about the project itself, so I can get a good feel for it."

"I don't know what else I can tell you," he said, frowning as he searched his mind for more details. "We've pretty much covered it."

"Have we?" She wished she'd gotten more details from Quinn. "Then tell me again how you want the press handled. Cleaning up the riverfront doesn't sound like a project that will need much manipulation of the press to generate a positive public response."

"Generally speaking, it shouldn't. But my brother, Jo— Peter . . ."

"Your brother's name is Jupiter?"

"No, ah, it's Peter. Peter. Anyway, we're concerned about those last two apartment buildings. I told you about them, remember? They still have tenants and the owner is refusing to sell?"

"Oh, right. I remember now. And how much are they holding out for?"

He frowned. For an obviously intelligent woman, her memory was surprisingly short. He wondered if it had anything to do with the amount of food she'd consumed.

"No. I told you earlier, money didn't have anything to do with it. We could have handled that. It's sentimental."

"Sentimental can be very tricky sometimes," she said, reaching for the crème brulée. She took a bite, savored it, then waved her spoon back and forth in the air. "Is it the people or the buildings?"

"Both, I think."

She glanced at him, then quickly back to her food. His dark eyes were focused on her chest—her overexposed chest.

She felt hot all over.

He was hesitant. "You know, I think we had this same conversation about thirty minutes ago."

This might have unraveled the average imposter, but the Asher triplets had been stepping in for one another since they were in kindergarten. In that time, they had developed a small book of rules and pat answers.

"Of course, we did," she said. "But I like to go over things a couple of times to be sure I have them straight."

People who knew the Asher sisters well could always detect their true identities because their body language, like their personalities, was so very different. Also, Corrie had a minute scar above her left eyebrow from a bicycle accident when they were seven. Quinn's hair went one step beyond curly to frizzy. And Katherine bit her nails. But to an unsuspecting stranger . . .

"Fair enough," he said. "But let's let it soak in for a while and go over it again some other time. Frankly, I'd much rather talk about you."

"Me?" She made the mistake of looking at him again. He drew his gaze from her décolletage to meet hers, and the impact was enough to curdle the thick creamy custard in her mouth.

"Did . . . didn't we talk about me earlier? Before we talked about the project?"

Quinn had more in common with both Katherine and Corrie than the sisters had with each other. Katherine and Corrie were polar opposites, and Quinn was like a healthy mix of the two. She always did all the personal stuff during a switch because she didn't have to pretend to know what she was talking about and was less likely to trip the other two up with a lie.

"Let's talk about you," she suggested eagerly, resisting the temptation to look down at her chest. She could fill the bodice of Corrie's dress as well as Corrie, and knew that her bosom was at least covered. She had no idea why he couldn't seem to keep from looking at it. It was as if he were confused or puzzled by it—which didn't seem likely in a man who wore his own sexuality as easily as other men wore jeans. "Your life must be terribly interesting, what with all the traveling you do. I think I remember reading about the renovations your firm did in St. Louis. You must have wonderful stories about the people you've met and the places you've been to."

"I've already told you the good ones, and the rest aren't fit for lively dinner discussion. A lot of legal hocus-pocus that'd bore you to tears."

This was where a switch could get complicated, and why there were rules.

No sister, acting on another's behalf, will inject her own likes or dislikes into a conversation if it isn't in the best interest of the original sister.

Katherine was a lawyer, but Corrie thought the American justice system sucked beans. It took too long, it cost too much, it wasn't fair and equal. . . . How many times had she had to listen to her sister's democratic drivel on the subject?

"Probably," she said, enjoying the *boules sur chocolat* that wouldn't exist if there were no just desserts, so to speak, for those who worked for them—like herself. "But your life can't be all business. Surely you must see and do fun things in the cities you work in. I mean, I don't think big cities are all alike, do you? Don't they all have their own special flavor and personality? It has to be fun for you to get to know each one."

"Actually, that's part of the job, too, though I admit it's not the worst part. We have to get to know the city, its history and customs, in order to blend our projects into the existing community. Something sleek and modern designed for Seattle would stick out like a sore, ugly thumb in New Orleans. And everything in the Southwest might as well come from a foreign country if you try to stick it in New York. You're right, though, the differences are interesting. Someday I'd like to have the chance to settle somewhere and put down roots."

"So, you don't like to travel," she said, feeling an instant link between them that the flighty Corrie wouldn't have.

"Well, it was okay when we were younger, when we first started out, but . . . no. I'm tired of traveling. I'd like to settle down, I think." He paused. "I built a house a couple of years ago. Outside San Francisco. It's just sitting there empty, waiting for me."

"Why can't you live there?" she asked, looking him straight on for the first time—and enjoying it tremendously. His hair had a shiny, healthy glow to it. It was cut conservatively, but had a natural wave that lent him a sort of wild, reckless air, which appealed to her—though wild and reckless weren't normally what she looked for in a man. "Couldn't you make San Francisco a home base or something? Go to wherever your next project is, check it out, then go home and plan it?"

"If I were married with children, I might. But that'd be tough. Each project can last up to five or six years, depending on the size of it, the support we get, the financiers. . . . We oversee the construction, too, so that would mean flying back and forth constantly. Right now it's easier just to move and then pack up and leave when it's over."

She could hear the dissatisfaction in his voice, and she sensed a deep loneliness in him that pulled at her heart.

"If you're unhappy with the way things are now, does that mean you might be planning a change?" She smiled. "A smaller firm maybe? Smaller projects?"

He smiled back, causing a wonderful disturbance directly below her breastbone. Then he shook his head. "Not really. I like what I do, and I do have my brother to consider."

"He likes to travel."

"He likes the excitement of a big project. He's the gung ho type. The bigger the better, you know? And no one city is going to have enough big jobs to keep him happy."

"I've heard that you can be a little gung ho yourself," she said, recalling Corrie's complaints of the pushy, arrogant, all-knowing, all-powerful, all-business man who couldn't possibly be the same man sitting next to her. "If fact, I've heard you can be down right . . . obnoxious, I think was the word."

He laughed. "Me? Obnoxious?" he asked. "Nah. I've been known to get a little steamed up about something, and once in a while I have to kick a few tails. But I'm never obnoxious." He paused, then added, "Now, my brother's the one who can get wired real easy, and he can be . . . oh, let's say abrasive, now and again."

She laughed, too, and said, "We have something in common, then. I have a sister like that, and people are constantly getting the two of us mixed up."

"Let's make a deal, then," he said, crossing his arms on the table and leaning toward her. "Don't believe everything you hear about me, and I won't believe everything I hear about you."

"Why? What have you heard about me?" she asked, ready to take notes and report it to Corrie.

"Not much."

"Come on. Tell me. I can take it."

"I heard that despite the fact that you have an incredible imagination and do the best PR around, you're also something of an emotionally disturbed space cadet."

"A what?"

"Someone who constantly screws things up and then has a fit when they aren't going her way. Overbearing and scatterbrained at the same time, which I don't think describes you at all."

No, but it fit Corrie like a wax mask.

"Thank you," she said, and because she liked him she added, "but I think I should warn you, I can be difficult at times."

"Well, if you get too difficult, I'll chalk it up to your artistic temperament." And sugar consumption, he thought as he watched her finish off the last dessert.

"You do that," she said, hoping he could, once he'd gotten to know Corrie better. She wished Quinn had thought to order coffee.

"Isn't it strange the way first impressions can be so wrong?" he said, glancing downward, well below her chin again. "I was dreading meeting you—meeting with you, I mean—again. But I'm really glad I came. I think we got off to a bad start in your office the other day."

If her sister was any judge, it couldn't have been a truer remark. Which meant Corrie would owe her sisters big time for rectifying his initial—and probably correct—judgment of her. Payback would be sweet, Katherine decided, never having enjoyed her sister's escapades.

"I think we did too," she said. "And I'm sorry about that." She grinned. "And I'm really glad you came tonight, because I'd have looked very strange sitting here eating three desserts all by myself."

"You wouldn't look strange eating anything," he said. Sexy as hell, but not strange, he thought. His eyes lowered fleetingly to her chest and back again as he spoke. "I don't know where you put it all."

She couldn't stand it anymore. His dark sweeping eyes had her lifting a self-conscious hand to her breast as a hot crimson flush rose up her neck and into her cheeks.

"I'm sorry," he said, looking truly contrite. Then he laughed. "Really. It's just that . . . well, I could be losing my mind, but I'd have sworn that pin was on the other side of your dress earlier."

Shaken a bit by his astute powers of observation, her fingers crawled to the golden cow with the provocative udders.

"Oh," she said, relieved and strangely disappointed that he hadn't been fascinated by her cleavage after all. "No. You're right. It was on the other side, but I changed it in the ladies' room. I thought it looked better on this side."

He sat back and considered it openly, much to her discomfort.

"It looks good on both sides," he said, raising his gaze warmly and suggestively to hers. "You're well balanced."

Corrie would have loved it. She'd have slapped her knee and come back with some snappy, lewd rejoinder that would have pleased him. Quinn would have laughed it off and let it go, maybe even taken it as a compliment. Katherine wanted to disappear. Pooph! Just like that.

Not because of what he'd said. She wasn't naive or prudish. She knew men. But because of the way he'd said it; because he clearly liked and wanted her body—which was never what she wanted a man to want or enjoy first about her. She knew of at least two other people with the exact same body, so it wasn't that big of a deal.

She wanted him to see and know and be attracted to the differences in her; to the way she felt, the way she thought, what she liked, what she dreamed about.

Hold it. She gave herself a mental shake. She wasn't Katherine; she was Corrie for all intents and purposes. And Corrie didn't care whose body she had so long as men liked it and it got her from one place to the next when she wanted it to.

"You're too kind," she said in a low, husky voice, forcing a cheeky smile as she fought off the resentment welling inside her. She wanted to be herself with this man. She wanted him to see *her*, know *her*, like *her*.

"I can be kinder," he said suggestively. "I know you'd rather jump out of airplanes or fall off bridges with rubber bands buckled to your ankles than do anything as dull and sedate as go boating, but I've had my baby shipped up from Texas and I'd love to take you out on her sometime. Boating can be very exciting."

"Like during a hurricane?" she asked, pretending to consider the adventure under certain circumstances. "Aren't those a little hard to special order just to impress a woman?"

He set his wineglass aside and leaned forward again. His head bent close to hers as he watched his index finger gently caress the warm, soft skin of her upper arm.

"I don't need a hurricane to impress a woman," he said, his voice low and intimate. The scent of his spicy aftershave tickled her nose. She breathed deeper and deeper until it filled her mind with pleasure and faraway thoughts. Chills of delight ran up and down her arm, heralding the promise of raptures soon to come.

"I know you don't," she murmured, already impressed. "But what about professionalism? You are a client of mine, you know. And lots of people advise against getting . . . too impressed by their clients."

No sister, acting on another's behalf, will commit the original sister to becoming sexually or emotionally involved.

It was a rule. One Katherine was glad to adhere to in this instance. Selfishly, if she couldn't become involved with John Wesley, she sure didn't want Corrie to.

"Are you saying you don't date your clients?"

"Pretty much."

"No exceptions?"

"A few exceptions." Michael had been a client at first. "But never important ones."

He took a brief break from the ardent study of her face to consider her value as a public relations manager versus firing her on the spot. He sighed deeply, smiled, and leaned back into the seat, gracefully admitting temporary defeat. He'd need her brain more than her body for a while, but once the project was underway . . .

"Okay," he said, grinning in a way that had her

heart racing like the pistons in the engine of a getaway car. "But I want you to know that I don't give up easily, and that guy you told me about earlier isn't going to phase me."

Her brows rose with interest. Quinn had told him about Michael, and he was still coming on to her?

"Well, what if he phases me?" she asked, more intrigued than insulted by his arrogance.

"He doesn't. Not the way he should, anyway."

True. Katherine wasn't in love with Michael, but Corrie wanted to be. She needed to proceed with some caution.

"Well, that's neither here nor there, and it's certainly nothing two professionals like us should be discussing, I think," she said, groping for her purse. "Look. I want to make something very clear before I go. I'm really excited about your project. It'll be good for the city, good for you, and good for me. I'm eager to work with you on it. But that's all I'm going to do with you. I . . . I may have done some things and said some things tonight that led you in the wrong direction, and I'm sorry. You're an interesting, intelligent, and very good-looking man, but I'm involved elsewhere. I shouldn't have let you think anything else."

He nodded affably. "That's the second time tonight you've given me that speech. I'm beginning to wonder who you're trying to convince, me or yourself."

"I know who I'm trying to convince, Mr. Wesley."

"I thought we'd settled on John. Me John, you Corrie, remember?"

That last comment had all the markings of a Quirky Quinlyn Quip. She cringed inwardly at his misconception that she, Katherine, would ever say such a thing.

"Okay, John. I just don't want to leave you with any misconceptions. I'm involved with someone."

"You live with him?"

"Yes."

"Are you going to have his baby?"

She gasped. "What?"

"It doesn't matter anyway," he said. There was a light in his eyes that scared her. Not the way a maniac's might scare her, but . . . well, it was hard to explain. She felt trapped. She felt as if he knew she was an imposter, as if he knew she was Katherine and he wanted her. Her, not Corrie, not Quinn. Her. Her throat grew tight as he continued to speak. "You're a puzzle, Corrie. A Chinese puzzle. Intricate, ingenious, obscure. I plan to put all the pieces together."

"All the pieces?"

He nodded, narrowing his eyes.

"You're like three different people," he said. Her eyes grew wide. Did he know? Was he angry? What would he do? Or . . . could he truly see her? Like a single pea under one of three identical shells, had he found her? "You can be a half-baked, hard-nosed business woman, and that's okay. You can be warm and friendly on the outside but private and reserved inside, then turn around in minutes and be cool on the outside and hotter than hell from within."

"And which personality do you like best?" she couldn't help asking.

"Each in it's own place and time, but I'm most attracted to this one."

"This one?" Who was he seeing? Corene? Quinlyn? Katherine?

"I'm going to break through the cool and get to the hot stuff." It was Katherine. It was her.

She shook her head and lowered her gaze from his. He'd already seen too much.

"I told you . . ."

"You told me you were involved. You didn't say how much involved."

"Very involved."

"You love him."

She looked straight into his eyes and dug deep for conviction and sincerity.

"Yes, I love him."

A knowing smirk twitched at his lips as he shook his head and said, "It's hard for you to lie, isn't it?"

"I'm not lying."

"You're not in love, either." His eyes narrowed again as he watched her. "At least, not with the man you're presently involved with."

Mayday! Mayday! She was in trouble, and she needed help.

"I think this has gone far enough," she said, clutching her purse like a shield as she slid to the edge of the seat. "I . . . I think we should put an end to this conversation before even a working relationship becomes impossible for us. Please, uh, call the office at your convenience, and we'll set up another time to get together on the river project. I'm looking forward to meeting your brother, Peter."

She was going to reach out and shake his hand, then changed her mind and stood to leave instead.

"Corrie." His voice was calm and smooth and deep, like a river could be when it hid dangerous currents and undertows and backwashes.

"Yes?"

"It's your eyes."

"What is?"

"All of it," he spoke slowly, letting every word pull her closer and closer to the banks of that river. "The heat. The lies. Everything you need. Everything you want. Everything I want to share with you. It's all there in your eyes."

She looked down at her purse. Her hands were shaking. What should she say? What could she say?

"Be careful driving home, John. Good night."

TWO

"He's a pompous, egocentric jerk," Corrie announced, flying high on the endorphins she produced naturally and simply with the rapid running of her mouth. "You should have seen him today. He took one look at me and started waltzing around my office as if he were the only client I had. He wants this and he wants that, and how soon can I get the demographics to him." She tapped her long crimson fingernails on Quinn's kitchen countertop. "I swear on next year's net profit, that if he had referred to *our little dinner the other night*, and how much I'd seemed willing to cooperate with him on this project, one more time, I would have . . . Just how willing was I the other night?"

Katherine and Quinn looked at each other and shrugged. They weren't sure. He didn't sound like the man they'd been with—and Corrie seemed to be a little over the edge that day, even for Corrie.

"You were politely willing," Katherine said, toying

absently with the pendant around her neck, her thoughts mired in the recollection of John Wesley's hands. She liked big, strong, capable-looking hands. "Nothing too strenuous."

That wasn't a nice thing to say, but she hadn't quite forgiven her sister for dragging her into the switch they'd pulled on the man with platter-sized hands, and shoulders that looked broad enough to support the world. She was usually much quicker to forgive and forget these things, but as he had been haunting her dreams at night and dancing on the fringes of her thoughts by day, her recovery period was a bit slow this time.

Still, she wasn't immune to Corrie's anxiety when she caught her slipping a hand into her purse to test the battery in her beeper. She felt a pang of guilt, and her heart softened when she realized that her sister was still agonizing over her relationship with Michael.

She looked up and caught Quinn's perceptive eye. Any man who caused their sister this much grief and undue concern wasn't going to get their vote for new brother-in-law.

"You're working awfully hard to keep him," Quinn said softly, making a statement and posing a question at the same time.

"It's dumb, isn't it?" she answered, not expecting an answer, not pretending to misunderstand. The sisters knew each other too well. "I can't believe I let him do things like this to me. I've been waiting all afternoon for his call." Because it was hard to face the pity in her sisters' eyes, she started rummaging through her purse. "Sometimes I think I'm overcompensating, you know? I'm working too hard to keep Michael, because I didn't work hard enough to keep Joey? Does that make sense?"

"Makes sense to us," Quinn said, nodding along with Katherine.

"But is he as much a keeper as Joey was?" Katherine asked. "We hardly know him. We rarely ever see him."

Corrie shrugged as she pulled an appointment book from the depths of her pocketbook.

"You make him nervous," she said, sounding oddly contrite. "It makes him feel strange to see my face three times in the same room."

Two sets of blue eyes met and exchanged a common thought.

As identical triplets, they were an oddity in themselves. Most triplets were fraternal and didn't look exactly alike. The chances of producing three identical babies from a single egg were about one in several hundred thousand. They'd been considered unusual since before they were born.

They were accustomed to people being curious about them, unsure of how to act around them, even suspicious of them at times. But they had long ago discovered their differences, and their parents had cultivated them, individualized their daughters until the only people they truly enjoyed being with were the people who took the time to get to know them separately.

Besides, how the rest of the world perceived them and felt about them was the rest of the world's problem. In this case, it was Michael's problem—only Corrie wasn't seeing it that way. Her "You make him nervous" spoke volumes on the effect Michael was having on her self-confidence. And while it hurt the other two to be wished away, they weren't without understanding. Each, in her own time, for her own reasons, had wished to have exclusive ownership of her face.

"More good news," she said a few minutes later as she hung up the phone, her voice a little too loud, a little too stressed. "Mr. Charming called and wants me to return his call tonight. Can you believe this guy? As if I don't have a life outside the office? Hell, I'm not going to do it." She returned the appointment book to her purse. "If he wants to talk with me, he can do it during office hours."

"What if it's important?" Quinn asked. The John Wesley she knew wouldn't have called otherwise.

"Maybe it can't wait until Monday," Katherine added, wanting to call him immediately, just to hear his voice once more.

Corrie considered this, then reluctantly removed the book from her bag again.

"Okay. I'm curious," she said, turning to the phone. "I'm dying to see what he thinks is so important. And it better be good. I'm in no mood for his games. . . . Hello. This is Corene Asher returning John Wesley's call."

Fifty minutes later . . .

"No. No. No. I said no, and I meant no," Katherine muttered to herself, stepping into the elevator in John Wesley's hotel. "So what happened? We never switch on the same person more than once. Too much can go wrong."

Quinn had agreed with her on that point. But Corrie had continued to cajole. Katherine had held firm for a good ten minutes before her youngest sister pushed her over the edge.

"I'd do it for you," she'd said sweetly, with tears of tension shimmering in her eyes.

"That's true," Quinn had agreed from her firm perch on the proverbial fence.

Now Katherine found herself facing the door to John Wesley's suite. "This is wrong. Ethically. Morally. It's unfair and dishonest and . . ." She knocked on the door.

"Mr. Wesley, this better be good," Katherine said, marching into a simple suite of rooms, à la Corrie. "I'm not in the habit of—"

She stopped dead in her tracks. A table for two was in the center of the room. Candles glowed warm and cozy and flowers spilled their sweet fragrance into the sung little trap he'd obviously gone to a great deal of trouble to set for her.

"I wanted to send you some flowers, but I didn't want your boyfriend coming over here to remove my liver with a ballpoint pen. This was the next best thing," he said from behind her, before she had a chance to say anything.

"I thought you said this meeting was vital," she said, too stunned to think of anything better.

"Okay. I had a vital need to give you flowers."

"What? Why?"

"Because you remind me of flowers. The way you smell. The softness of your skin."

"Flowers? I remind you of flowers?" she asked, turning on him to hide her panic with a mild display of insult. "Is that the best you could come up with? Flowers? Every man in the world uses flowers."

"But I'm not every man in the world."

"No, you're not." If her jittering nerves and sweaty palms were any sort of indicator, he might very well have been the only man in the world. "I think I should leave."

"Don't you like flowers?"

"Sure I do, but . . . but not like this. I told you. I'm already involved with someone."

"Why do you keep using that word, 'involved'? Why don't you tell me you're in love with him?"

"I already have, several times, but okay, I'm in love with him."

"With feeling."

She glared at him.

"Look," she said, trying to be reasonable and not notice the size of his hands at the same time. "I appreciate the flowers, but I'm in . . . taken, and this is all wrong."

He glanced around the room, frowning. "Why is it wrong? Did I forget something? Oh! The music."

"Stop." She blocked his path to the stereo equipment with a single hand to his chest. She removed it immediately. "Please, don't do this."

When his gaze lowered and penetrated hers, she looked away.

"I just want to talk. That's all."

"About what?"

"You. I want to know you."

"No."

"Why not? If you're really in love with this other guy, I'm no threat to either of you, right? How can talking hurt?"

"We can talk at the office on Monday."

"We don't seem to be able to get along at your office."

"That's true," she said, momentarily defeated by fact. "You're not very nice at the office."

"Well, let's say . . . I'm somebody else at the office. Away from the office we get along pretty well, don't you think? Like the other night at dinner?"

"Then we should talk in a park or on the street or in a crowded restaurant. But not here. Not like this."

"Does knowing there's a bed in the next room make you nervous?"

"Yes. No. Of course not."

A shrewd smile came to his lips, and her disguise withered a little.

"You're too pretty to lie," he said softly. She could all but feel his mouth at her neck, and he was a good two feet away. Her heart skipped with anticipation.

"Will you stop fibbing if I promise not to touch you? Until you want me to, that is."

"I'm not going to want you to touch me," she warned him, picturing her teeth rotting and turning black in the wake of her lie.

"Okay. But no more lies."

She was a lie, therefore she couldn't commit herself.

"Have you eaten?" he asked.

"No." It was an easy answer.

"Great. I was hoping I'd caught you in time." He'd ordered a small truckload of food from room service and had planned to open a delicatessen if she'd already eaten, though with her appetite . . .

He sighed and rubbed his hands together, eager for another night of pure erotica in watching her eat. "Would you like some wine while we wait?"

"Sure." Gallons of it, she thought. Switching on him was all wrong. Once in an emergency was understandable. Twice was too deceitful. "So, what shall we talk about?"

"You."

"We did that."

"Okay," he said, sitting down on the couch. "As I recall, we covered recreation and business. Now tell me about your family, your background."

"Why?" She sat *way* on the other end of the couch, on the edge, ready to leave at any time.

"Because I want to know. Tell me anything you want to tell me."

"I have two sisters," she said, wishing one of them to the devil.

"Older or younger."

"Younger." Which was true if she was Katherine, but as Corrie . . . "I mean older. I'm the youngest."

"And one of them's a lawyer, right?"

"Katherine. How did you know that?"

"Her name came up the other day, and I asked if the two of you were related."

"Came up where?"

"Over a bottom-line business lunch. It seems we may have a little conflict-of-interest problem involving those last two buildings."

"In what way?"

"Well," he said, stretching his legs out and laying a lazy arm across the back of the couch—he could almost touch her shoulder with the tips of his fingers. "As it happens, it turns out that your sister is the owner's lawyer."

"Who's the owner?"

"A little old lady by the name of Gumph."

"Belle Gumph?" she asked, sick from the sinking sensation in her chest.

"You know her?"

"I've . . . heard of her. She scares my sister to death on a twice-a-month schedule."

He grinned. "She scares me too. I met with her this afternoon, and she had me shaking in my boots."

"You saw Belle, uh, Mrs. Gumph this afternoon about her buildings, without my sister?"

"She said she didn't want to bring in her big guns till she needed them," he said, amused. "Is she really a barracuda?"

"Who? Me, ma . . . my sister? Katherine? No."

Oh, Lord. There was compost in the central air ducts now. If Belle Gumph refused to cooperate with the city government and give up her buildings peaceably—which, if Katherine were a betting woman, would be her call—they'd be forced to claim them in eminent domain and Belle would fight them.

They'd go to court. John would be there. He'd see her and know she wasn't Corrie. She'd be brought up on ethics charges and disbarred. . . . Or worse yet, Belle could find out that she'd been consorting in the enemy camp, lash her with her tongue until she bled, and *then* drag her in on ethics charges and have her disbarred. Either way, her career would be over.

"Katherine does what has to be done," she said, feeling her first obligation was to Belle—and not because the old lady scared the begeebees out of her. "She's good, but I wouldn't call her a barracuda. She's not ruthless."

"According to the old lady, if we forced her to call Katherine Asher in on this, we may not live long enough to rue the day. She says your sister will chew us up and spit us out like a worthless piece of gristle."

She shrugged, pleased indeed with such high praise. She couldn't help but smile.

He smiled too. "And if that wasn't enough to discourage us," he said with raised brows, "she went on to confide that the reason your sister never married is, in part, due to the fact that most men are afraid of her. She intimidates them and browbeats them into whimpering . . . ah, what was it? . . . whiny, worthless wimps, or something equally appealing. And she reminded us that there wasn't an animal in the world more fierce than a bitter spinster with a sharp brain and a set of law books."

Katherine stared at him, speechless. He began to chuckle.

"I'm relieved to see that you don't recognize that description of your sister."

"I . . . I'm . . . stunned. I . . . Katherine isn't at all like that. I . . . She's . . . she's . . ."

"Like you?"

"What?" Her voice broke in sudden panic.

"She's like you. Hardworking. Ambitious. Dedicated. My brother and I weren't particularly impressed with ol' Belle's scare tactics, but just to play it safe, we checked with our own lawyer. He said she was highly respected and easy to work with."

Relieved, she sighed loudly and took a sip of wine.

Watching her, he smiled and noted, "You're proud of your sister's reputation."

"Sure. She's earned it. The, uh, highly respected and easy-to-work-with one, I mean." Did they make muzzles for old women? she wondered, picturing Belle in one such fine device.

"And you're close."

"The three of us are very close."

"Tell me about your other sister."

"That's Quinlyn. Quinn, we call her."

"What do you call Katherine? Kathy? Kate?"

"No. We call her Katherine. Nicknames don't stick to her very well, you know? She's . . ."

"Slick?"

"No." She laughed.

"Stuffy?"

"No."

"Snooty?"

"She's just Katherine." Why didn't she have a nickname? "She's always been Katherine."

"Okay. And what does Quinn do?"

"She's married to a contractor and has three kids. She taught kindergarten before she had twins," she said, taking a risk in mentioning the twins.

"Twins? Do twins run in your family?" he asked, with a guarded expression.

Multiple births were generally hereditary, and he obviously knew this. If she told the truth, would he guess at their deception? Maybe not. After all, she thought, she'd never see him again. Except in court, perhaps, and by then he'd know Corrie better than he knew her.

"My mother was a twin," she said, after a brief hesitation. "Does that make you nervous? That someone you're sitting this close to is capable of having more than one baby at a time?"

His reserve was quickly gobbled up with amusement as he said, "Nothing about you makes me nervous, except maybe what I'll find under that cool, aloof shell of yours."

"There is no shell," she said, lowering her gaze to her wineglass. "I am what you see. Nothing more. Nothing less." To quote Corrie, she added, "I'm honest and up-front with people because it saves me a lot of time."

"At the office," he said, watching her closely. Too closely. "But alone, away from the office, you're different."

"I thought that was you," she said with a lopsided smile. "The split personality. One for work, one for play."

Taken aback by the reminder, he nodded sheepishly. "I'll have to work on that."

"Well, I'm no peach either," she said, knowing firsthand the amount of irritation her sister could generate. "We'll both work on it." Her lawyer's timing stepped in. "Katherine says that once a settlement has been reached, you hustle out of the courtroom before anything can go wrong with it. So I think now would be a good time for me to leave."

"But you just got here," he said, standing with her. "And dinner's on its way up."

"Oh. Right," she said weakly, shifting her weight, impatient to be gone. She knew she should get as far away from his dark probing eyes and the raw male sexuality he exuded as she possibly could. "Well, I guess . . . you know, I'm really not all that hungry. I had a late lunch with a client and—"

"I haven't asked all my questions yet. And you said you'd stay for dinner if I didn't touch you. I haven't broken my promise, have I?"

A resigned sigh escaped her.

"No," she said, deciding to make the best of the situation. "But let's talk about you instead."

"Fair enough," he said, taking her wineglass to add more to what she'd barely touched. "Ask me anything."

"All right. Where are you from originally? Is it just you and your brother, or are there more siblings? Where did you go to school? What's your political persuasion? Do you hate to wear ties?"

He was laughing. "Whoa. Let me see now. . . . Milwaukee; yes and no; Stanford; bipartisan; and yes, I hate to wear ties."

"Very good," she said, laughing easily. "Now your favorite color and number, where you were last New Year's Eve, your most embarrassing moment, your happiest moment, and . . . and the name of the first girl you kissed."

After their meal had been delivered, he served her from silver covered dishes while he regaled her with his memories. He spoke often of his brother, Peter, as if they'd shared many of the same memories as youngsters, carefully pointing out the differences in their character and personalities, though, strange as it seemed to Katherine, Peter sounded more like John than John sometimes.

Peter was the laid-back, highly imaginative sort

who preferred drawing and doodling at his drafting board to the aggressive sales-and-management end of the practice, which he left primarily to John, though at times it took both of them doing both jobs to pull off a specific project.

He and his brother had shared a happy childhood, his parents still lived in the same house in Milwaukee, and for all intents and purposes, John Wesley didn't seem to have a thing in the world to complain about or hide. It was a pure joy to listen to someone talk about his life as if it were something he was satisfied with and grateful for. Even his love life seemed relatively unmarred by unhappiness.

Neither brother had found the time to marry, being too busy building their company and its reputation to think of such things. They seemed to enjoy short, sweet entanglements to anything long-term or involving any sort of commitment.

"Sometimes, lately, I've wondered if it's worth it," he said, picking up her wineglass, leading her back across the room to the comfort of the couch, into a warm golden world of candlelight. "Being successful doesn't make up for the nights when you can't sleep and there's no one around to talk to. Money can be a burden more than anything else, if there's no one around to spend it on. And fame doesn't always mean much if there's no one around to be proud of you."

"I know," she said quietly.

This time he cleverly chose to let her sit first, so that he was free to sit as close to her as he wanted.

"Is that why you're *involved*, with that guy? So you'll have someone to share your success with?" he asked, taking a thick lock of her dark hair between his fingers, examining its texture thoughtfully.

"I'm not involved," she said. "I mean, I'm not *just* involved with him. I love him."

He let her hair slip gently from his fingers, then tapped the tip of her nose.

"How come your nose doesn't grow when you lie like that?"

"Please, don't start that again."

"Then tell the truth."

Truth to tell, she was attracted to John Wesley like a magnet to a refrigerator. Physically he took her breath away. He had her nerves humming like taut piano wires. But in her mind he was even more attractive. He was like a rock island in a turbulent sea. Strong, firm, sure. Of course, she didn't know all there was to know about him, but his wholesome outlook on life was profoundly refreshing. No deep-seated phobias or phrenias. Nothing to prove to anyone. He was what he was—and he liked himself. She liked him.

"Okay. Michael and I have a few problems," she said. No lie there. "That doesn't mean I can drop everything and jump into bed with you."

He nodded his satisfaction, but wasn't taking any joy in it.

"I like loyalty. And . . . I'm sorry," he said. "Not because you're having trouble, but because it's hurting you."

What hurt was lying to him. She wanted to tell him she was as free as a look at a summer sky. She wanted to touch him. She wanted him to kiss her. She couldn't do any of those things posing as Corrie, and as Katherine she would never have the opportunity. That's what hurt.

"You know, this place has a pretty nice piano bar in the lobby. Would you like to go down for a drink and a dance?" he asked, sensing her despondency.

"Thanks," she said, smiling. And because he truly seemed to care about her and what he thought was her floundering love affair, she added, "Thanks for everything, but I think I should go. It's been nice. I'm glad I came."

"I'm glad you came too. Will I have to trick you again to get you to come back?"

"Probably," she said with a smaller smile. "Nothing's really changed between us, you know. We'll both be poops at work on Monday, and it'll be as if tonight never happened."

"What if we're not?" he asked, as if he were forming a plan of some kind in the back of his mind. "What if I show up at the office like this"—he put a hand on his chest—"and you come, not like a dragon lady, but gentle and thoughtful and beautiful and easy to talk to, the way you are now."

She sighed and shook her head. "I don't mean to be a dragon lady, John," she said in her sister's defense. "I'm . . . easily excited and I get wrapped up in things sometimes. Too wrapped up, maybe. But

I'll try. I'd really like for us to have a good working relationship."

"Too."

"Too?"

"Also. You want us to have as good a working relationship as we have a personal relationship."

She frowned. Did she? And how personal was personal? Friends? Lovers? Who was she kidding? She knew exactly what he wanted. And what she wanted. The air fairly sparked from the friction of their needs and desires rubbing together. But she knew, too, that what they wanted wasn't to be. For as Corrie, she wouldn't cheat on Michael, and as Katherine, she couldn't dupe John—or betray herself.

She sighed and decided to take a wild stab at "friends" and let Corrie handle whatever came back on the fork. Katherine had had enough.

"Of course I do. Being friends will make everything easier for both of us."

"Great," he said, standing, extending a hand to her. "So how about that dance now?"

She took his hand. It was warm and strong and full of electrical currents that went shooting up her arm as she came to her feet. She released it immediately.

"I should go."

"Probably. But it's still early," he said, clearly reluctant to let her leave. "How's this? One more hour, one dance, one kiss, and then you go. And I'll try not to cry when I wave good-bye."

She laughed at his silliness—and because talking about kissing made her feel a little light-headed.

"How about half an hour and one dance?" she said, a born litigator.

"One drink, one dance, one kiss—five minutes each—fifteen minutes tops."

It sounded like a good deal to Katherine, but . . .

No sister, acting on another's behalf, will engage in any intimacies whatsoever with the unknowing, regardless of the unknowing's relationship with the original sister.

She'd insisted on that rule herself to keep from having to kiss or do more with Quinn's husband, Robert, in college when they were first dating. Of course, he'd spotted the switch right off and he'd been furious with them, but the rule had remained intact.

"No kissing," she said with a shake of her head, too full of regret to think that she might not be hiding it well.

"One kiss and a rain check for the drink and the dance."

Again she laughed. "No deal."

"You're curious," he said, baiting her. He was so sure of his statement that to deny it would be calling him a liar. And they both knew which of them had the tendency toward skirting the truth.

"So I'm curious," she said. "I'm curious about space travel, but that doesn't necessarily mean I'm hopping on the next shuttle."

"Outer space could be the thrill of your life. It could be what you were meant for, your destiny."

"I get dizzy looking out of airplane windows. I'd never make it in space." She was aware that his hands had come to rest on either side of her waist; it felt as if they were burning holes through her dress. She met his gaze and, in prompt retrospection, decided it was a major mistake.

"I . . . Did I say I wanted you to touch me?" she asked, referring to his predinner promise. Her every heartbeat was like cannon fire reverberating through her body.

"Your eyes did," he said, his breath warm on her lips. His eyes were so close and so dark, she felt her next ragged breath would send her plummeting into their depths, never to be seen or heard from again.

"I . . . I have a slight astigmatism. Maybe you misunderstood them."

Humor sparked in his expression and he smiled. Slowly he closed the circle of his embrace.

"Maybe you're wishing misunderstood," he said, his lips brushing hers lightly, gently like the fingers of a pickpocket, ready to steal away her every penny's worth of restraint.

The breath she'd been holding escaped her with a shudder. She tried to swallow her own cravings, but they stuck in her throat, solid and aching. Her heart fluttered in alarm. When he took her lower lip between his, sucking and nibbling softly, her eyes closed.

A moan that signaled nothing but pleasure and long-awaited satisfaction echoed in her ears. That the sound had come from her mattered not at all, for he deepened the kiss, and she was lost in a world of color and light.

The complicated became simple. And passive resistance was quickly overcome by raging passions and needs.

Her hands roamed free across his broad shoulders. Searching, discovering, reveling. Power and strength coiled and curled beneath her fingertips. His neck was warm; the muscles were as taut as steel fetters controlling something wild and primitive. Engorged and aching, her breasts sought comfort against his chest while she indulged her senses in his taste, his smell, the thick softness of his hair, and the magnificent chaos in the conflict between the gentleness of his lips and ruthlessness of his tongue.

He pulled away a little too soon for her liking. She leaned closer, trying to reengage the splendid sensations.

He taunted her, barely brushing his lips against hers. "The deal was one kiss."

She frowned.

"I think you're in big trouble," he said, his mouth skimming over her cheek, her furrowed brow, her jaw.

"I know I am," she murmured, a blurry image of Corrie rippling through her mind.

"When are you going to tell him?"

"Him?" She opened her eyes. Another major mistake, she realized, as the world came rushing back to greet her like a punch in the gut.

"Your boyfriend. You can't kiss me like that and still think you're in love with him."

"I can't kiss you, period," she said, stepping back, appalled. "I am so sorry. I shouldn't have done that."

"I kissed you first," he reminded her, amused by her reaction.

"I shouldn't have let you," she said, glancing around for her purse. "And I shouldn't have kissed you back. I'm so sorry."

"Corrie, stop. Please," he said, hustling to reach the door before she did. "Sharing a kiss isn't such a bad thing. We were both curious, and now we know."

"Yes. Now we know. Know what?" she asked, flummoxed, stopping several feet from the door just as he got to it.

"That there's something special between us. Something bigger and better than what you have with that other guy."

"Ho-hold it right there," she said, still out of breath. "What I have with Michael is no concern of yours. I've told you that before. And I mean it. I'm sorry if I gave you the wrong impression with that kiss, but like you said, it was no big thing. Let's forget it ever happened."

"No way," he said. "And I said it wasn't a bad thing—it was definitely a big thing. A really big thing. A huge thing. And I'm not settling for just one."

"You're going to have to," she said, boldly taking several steps forward. "I'd like to leave now."

"This isn't over, Corrie."

"Yes it is." Every time he called her Corrie, it was more and more over. She hated it when he called her Corrie. "Move away from the door."

He did so, but slowly and without taking his gaze off her.

"Monday is a long way off. If you need to talk, I'll be here all weekend," he said, watching her fumble with the door handle.

"Maybe you should get out more," she muttered as the door came open.

"Maybe you should stop lying. To me. To yourself. To him."

Her soaring emotions touched down in anger. She was angry with herself for adding injury to insult to his deception. Angry with him for being handsome and smart and wonderful and honest and just about everything else she wanted in a man. Angry with Corrie for dating Michael, who was an incredible loser and the cause of the most miserable night of her—Katherine's—life. Angry with Quinn for being Corrie's sister . . . the list went on.

"Well, *maybe* you should mind your own business," she said, lashing out at the only person on her list that she could get to then. "It could be a novel experience for you."

"Well, *maybe* I am minding my own business," he said in a like tone before it dropped a few octaves and he added, "And you are a novelty for me."

"Then you really do need to get out more," she

said, stepping into the hall and closing the door firmly between them.

She half walked, half ran to the elevator, hands trembling, tears threatening.

THREE

"It just happened. I knew it was coming. I saw it coming. I should have been prepared for it, but I wasn't," a still-agitated Katherine said, early Monday morning in Corrie's office. "It happened. I'm sorry. But you're going to have to deal with it. I'm out of it. One switch per customer has always been more than enough in the past, and I think this proves that twice is too many. In fact, I don't ever want to switch with you again. We're adults now. It's time we grew up. I don't care how desperate you get, don't ask me to switch ever again. Or Quinn either."

Silence gravitated through the room like a low-lying cloud.

"So?" Corrie asked, looking for all the world only mildly curious.

"So?" Katherine repeated, surprised her sister wasn't bouncing off the walls by now.

"How was it?"

"How was what?"

"The kiss."

"Well, ah, um . . ." She raised her brows and hands in a vague, disjointed manner, wholly unprepared for the question. "It was okay."

"Just okay?"

"Nice."

"Nice?"

"Very nice."

Corrie nodded and glanced away, concealing her thoughts—which was always a bad omen.

"Forget it."

"Forget what?" she asked, putting on an innocent expression—another foreboding signal.

"Whatever you're thinking, forget it. I don't want to see or hear about that man again as long as I live. Understand?"

"Fine," she said, giving in far too easily for her sister's peace of mind. "I appreciate you filling in for me, and I'll handle it from here."

"Aren't you mad about the kiss?"

"Stuff happens," she said, casually shuffling through the papers on her desk, still carefully avoiding her sister's discerning gaze. "Besides, the way you follow rules, I'm sure that it couldn't have been anything more than an accident. How could I get mad about an accident?"

By definition, an accident was an unfortunate event resulting from carelessness, ignorance, or unavoidable causes. Since Katherine was aware of her attraction to

John Wesley and certainly not ignorant of what could come of such an attraction and therefore should have avoided the situation altogether, she was feeling no little gratitude for her sister's magnanimous attitude. However . . .

"What's wrong?" she asked, watching Corrie closely. "What's happened? Where were you all weekend?"

"Dumping Michael," she said, using a cocky attitude to hide her bruised and battered ego.

It didn't require the cellular bond between them for Katherine to feel her sister's deep pain and depression. She really wanted to say she was sorry, but she wasn't. Michael was the sort of bad news that belonged on the bottom of a bird cage.

However, there was a certain protocol to follow in the wake of an emotional disaster. Thankfully, therapy was therapy in her estimation, and the telling of the story was just as cathartic told as a comedy as it would have been if told as a tragedy.

"What happened?"

"He was with another woman."

"You saw her . . . and him . . . together?"

"I'd told him I'd be at the office all afternoon on Saturday and to call when he got home. I guess he lost track of the time."

"Oh no." Corrie wasn't the most organized person in the world, but she had an exacting temper, one of the few character traits she shared with both her sisters. "What did he say?"

"He didn't say anything. I didn't either. It was one of those moments when words weren't really necessary, you know? But he was so surprised to see me, he sat there in the bed while I poured the rest of the wine they'd been drinking on his clothes."

"Really?" She couldn't help the gleeful grin on her face.

"Hers too. Unfortunately, he sort of snapped out of it when I threw the empty bottle at him. He jumped out of bed naked and grabbed me, so I had to do what came natural," she said with a shrug.

"Oh no." Katherine groaned, her eyes twinkling merrily as she recalled the self-defense classes she'd insisted they all take, and how Corrie had excelled at a certain technique guaranteed to bring a man to his knees.

She started to laugh. When Corrie joined in a few seconds later, she sensed a full and rapid recovery dawning in her sister's heart. She was still chuckling when she stepped out of the elevator a short time later, on her way to her own office.

"You look happy this morning," John Wesley noted, his polite smile not quite reaching his eyes. They stood facing each other with briefcases in hand. Her palms became clammy with the urge to touch him. He, however, looked a little perturbed. "I suppose you've forgotten that we have an early appointment this morning."

"I haven't forgotten anything," she said, automatically stepping into Corrie's shoes. She didn't like the tone of his voice, but preferred to think that he might not be a morning person, rather than the Jekyll-and-Hyde character Corrie insisted he was. "I left something in my car, and I'll be back in my office before you even get there. Excuse me."

"Are you all right?" John asked, his eyes narrowing as he inspected her. She looked at him. He wasn't as concerned for her as he was confused by her cheery attitude, which struck a discordant note on her heartstrings.

They had discussed the fact that they were like different people in the workplace—and technically, she *was* a different person. But that he could be so different; so cool and detached after the kiss they'd shared two days earlier . . . well, it hurt. And it perplexed her.

Maybe the kiss hadn't affected him the way it had her. Maybe he hadn't been thinking about it all weekend or remembering the softness of her lips or the sweet taste of her mouth, the way she had his. Maybe he was pouting because she hadn't stayed with him. Maybe it hadn't made a bit of difference to him one way or the other. Maybe he was a Jekyll and Hyde.

"I'm fine," she said, and then because she knew he didn't really care, she added, "Thanks so much for asking."

"Don't be long. I have other things to do today," he said over his shoulder as he stepped into the elevator.

"Eat dirt and die," she muttered, stepping into the revolving door and out onto the sidewalk. "Sic him good, Corrie."

With the burden of John's kiss off her chest, so to speak, Katherine felt somewhat freer to purge the rest of her guilt for what she'd done—even though the impression of it was still hot on her lips and deep in her heart.

The switches were wrong, and they all three knew it. But not to use their unique advantage from time to time would be as wasteful as ignoring psychic powers or a natural talent for singing or art.

No, she thought, hissing when she burned her lip with hot coffee. That was rationalizing, not admitting fault and taking responsibility—the only true way to cleanse one's conscience.

She began again.

Every time they pulled a switch, they meddled with their own destinies. People and experiences meant for one of the sisters could be overlooked or neglected by one of the others. Opportunities taken by one, wouldn't even be seen by the others. It was as dangerous as it was useful. Well, useful in a fleeting, cheating sort of way, like a padded bra or plastic fingernails, she thought. Illusions that were temporarily effective, but hardly advantageous in the long run.

She did some heavy-duty calculating over the fresh garden salad she was having for lunch. Adding it all together and subtracting a tad, the answer always came out the same. No one had been hurt this time. Dented a little, maybe, but not hurt.

Corrie had kept her appointment with an important client and made a good impression, a better impression than she normally would have, as a matter of fact. John Wesley got to know more about Corrie, did a little flirting, and was told in no uncertain terms that she was spoken for—whether he wanted to believe it or not. Quinn had gotten a free meal and she hadn't had to do the dishes afterward. All in all, it had turned out fairly well for everyone . . . except perhaps herself.

Men who could take your breath away with a glance and make your pulse race at ultrasonic speed with the mere thought of their touch, didn't come along every day. Likable men who aroused sleeping emotions and touched tender places in the heart, who were tuned in to your thoughts and seemed to know you better than you knew yourself . . . Men like that were rare.

That John Wesley was one such man had been exciting and scary and wonderful, for one night. But that's all it was. One night . . . well, two really. No more than a few hours though. She'd never see him again.

And John? Well, if he had seen something in her eyes that he was attracted to, something that he wanted, he'd be looking in Corrie's eyes from now on and he wouldn't see it anymore. He might even start to believe that he'd been mistaken, Katherine thought, sadly acquiescent to the price the fates were demanding for her deception as she walked slowly back to her office.

"Well, hello!" It was John Wesley again. He was standing at the entrance to her building. And he was delighted to see her. "Did we agree to do this together? Or are you afraid the barracuda will eat me alive?"

"What?" Her mouth opened and closed several times before any more words came out. "What are you doing here?"

He looked stricken for a second, but recovered quickly. "I guess I must have told you I'd be sending my brother over here, but, well, I changed my mind and decided to come myself."

"To meet my sister?"

"Yep. Belle's big gun is shootin' blanks. Turning down our third offer for those buildings was a big mistake. But because she's your sister, I thought I'd come over and get her to rethink our offer before we're forced to bring in our own artillery."

"Rethink it. Aha."

"If I'd known you were planning to do the same thing, we could have had lunch together," he said with a grin, reaching for and holding the heavy glass door open for her. "I'm really glad you decided to come. I bet I forgot to tell you how pretty you looked this morning. You're even more beautiful now."

Feeling as punch-drunk as an old boxer, she stared at him, dumb and senseless. Who was this man? Not the snarling beast from Corrie's office that morning.

And who was she? Corrie, she guessed. And they were on their way up to see her . . . Katherine.

"Are you all right?" he asked, leaning close with genuine concern. "You look a little pale."

Just pale? Not transparent?

"No. I'm fine. I'm swell. I'm . . . great. Just great," she said, walking past him into the building, wishing she could get her trembling hands on Corrie's neck. "I was just thinking of something else, and I hadn't expected to see you. You surprised me a bit is all."

He was grinning happily when she glanced at him.

"I know the feeling," he said. "Every time I see you, I feel as if I've been hit by a Mack truck, only there's no pain. Just the impact and this overwhelming feeling that it's great to be alive."

Well, he had the Mack truck part right.

"Yes. Well . . . actually, I came to warn you about my sister," she said, words spewing forth as quickly as they crossed her mind.

He smiled. "That's really sweet of you, but I've dealt with lawyers before. I can handle your sister, Corrie."

Irksome as his arrogance was, she was more concerned with his discovering that he'd already handled Corrie's sister—intimately.

"That's not what I came to warn you about. Her secretary called my office, hoping to reach you, but you'd left. I guess there was some sort of emergency, a pressing legal matter Katherine needed to attend to, and she wasn't sure she'd be back in her office for your appointment and . . . and we couldn't seem to reach you by phone to head you off, and I had an appointment down this way anyway, so I thought I'd try to intercept you, save you the time of going up to her office just to find out she isn't there. And, well, she isn't up there."

"Maybe she's back," he said, pushing the elevator button.

"She's not."

"How do you know?"

"I just called—from my car—not two minutes ago to see if she was back and, uh, whether or not I should still try and head you off." She paused to play her words back in her mind, then added, "She wasn't back yet."

He looked disappointed, but accustomed to such setbacks. "Then I'll go up and make another appointment for tomorrow."

"I'll do that," she said hastily. "I was going up anyway, to drop off something . . . something personal and, um, I'd be glad to make the appointment for you."

The elevator arrived.

"Tell you what," he said, his gaze roving over her face as if he had nothing better to do and nothing could please him more. "You drop off your something personal, and I'll make my appointment, then the two of us'll slip out and play hooky for the rest of the afternoon."

She walked into the empty elevator because she didn't know what else to do.

"I can't. Hooky is out of the question," she said firmly.

"What for?"

"What for?" Corrie was right. The man was impossible. "Charming and handsome as you are, you're not the only client I have, you know. I can't just take an afternoon off any time I want. I have a business to run, employees to pay, a zillion things to do . . . and . . . and our professional relationship aside, there's still the matter of the man I'm living with. Now, I know we've established the fact that you and I are very much attracted to each other, but I can't go off and play hooky with you while I'm still living with Michael, now can I?"

His eyes were twinkling. His lips quirked with a smirk as he repeated his original question, *"What floor?"*

She squeezed her eyes closed. She'd admitted he was charming, handsome, and attractive for nothing— and he was acting like a cat in a dairy barn.

"Now don't get all huffy," he said, chuckling as he watched her jab at the button twice before she hit it. "I like a woman who cuts straight to the chase."

"What chase? There is no chase. There's not going to be any chase."

He shook his head good-naturedly.

"Sounds to me as if the only thing that's holding us up here is that you're living with a man you don't love."

She took a deep breath and opened her mouth to

protest, but he turned and laid a single finger to her lips, leaning close and speaking softly.

"Now, you don't impress me as the sort of woman who'd live with a man once she's figured out that she doesn't really love him. So I suspect he'll be leaving soon. And when he's gone, I'll have a green light. There most certainly will be a chase." He smiled with kindness and good humor. "And you won't stand a chance."

The authority and certainty in his words and manner seemed to suck all the air from the elevator. She tried to swallow, but couldn't. It was hard to breathe.

It took her several seconds to realize that the elevator had stopped, the doors had opened, and he was walking away from her. She had to step lively to beat him to the receptionist's desk.

"Ms. Asher," the terribly efficient Jean Graham greeted her with a friendly smile. "You have messages, several urgent ones from your sister Corrie."

When Katherine refused to take the pink missives from her outstretched hand, the woman looked to John Wesley and then back to Katherine in confusion.

John, too, began to frown and look bewildered.

Katherine started to laugh.

The sound was as nervous as it was forced, but it did take the furrow from John's brow, and he smiled back at her.

"People do this all the time," she said, and then turning to the firm's longtime employee with wide, expressive eyes, she went on, "You're the wonderful new receptionist my sister was telling me about. Joan or Jean, maybe?"

"Jean . . . Graham," the woman said, wary and watchful.

"Well, don't feel silly, Jean. People mix Katherine and me up all the time. I think it's the hairstyle, myself. Katherine's so much thinner than I am, and much more elegant and sophisticated, of course. I'm Katherine's sister Corrie, by the way. But we have the same color hair and we both wear it to our shoulders, and there is a family resemblance of sorts, don't you think?"

"Yes. Yes, I see the resemblance," Jean said. She, who never missed Corrie's long painted nails when she called on her sister—who, by the by, had a tendency to chew hers to the quick. "I'm pleased to meet you."

"Actually, we met on the phone. It's a little late for these," she muttered, taking the messages. Then, on second thought, she returned those not from Corrie. "This is John Wesley, Jean."

"How do you do, Mr. Wesley. Your appointment—"

"—had to be canceled. We know," Katherine broke in with a tilt of her head and a grimace of pure regret. "I've already told him how sorry Katherine was to have to cancel on short notice, and he's been very understanding. He'd like another appointment."

"Of course," she said without question. "When is a convenient time for you, Mr. Wesley?"

He shrugged. "I'm easy."

Not according to Corrie, Katherine thought. Not when it came to doing business. Now was not a good time to start being easy. He needed to give specific dates and times, she decided, so that she could come up with specific excuses to avoid him.

"You know," she said, lighting up like a fifty-watt bulb in a hundred-watt socket. "Why don't we make Katherine reschedule your appointment? She's the one who canceled, and we don't want to look too easy or too willing to cooperate with her."

He wasn't sure about this. "Do you think that's a good idea? Rescheduling an appointment isn't a problem. And, to a certain extent, I am willing to cooperate with her. I don't want to get her back up if I can avoid it."

"Listen. I know my sister," she said in earnest. "If you're too nice, she won't respect you, and if she doesn't respect you, she'll walk all over you with her boots on. Trust me. She's a lawyer. And she is my sister. You give her an inch of space, and she'll fill the riverfront project so full of holes, it'll sink the minute it hits the water."

"She's that tough?" He looked a little ill.

"Personally, she's a peach. Professionally, well, let's just say she's . . . uh, she's . . ."

"A slick operator?" Jean offered helpfully, an astute twinkle in her eyes.

Katherine nodded, lowering her eyes sheepishly. "Slick operator," she muttered.

Truth to tell, she was feeling less and less like

the slick, shrewd, and clever Katherine and more and more like the reckless, mercurial, and scattered Corrie these days.

He released a resigned sigh.

"I don't want to play hardball with your sister," he said, his somber gaze showing no fear, his reluctance being purely personal. "But if you think that's the best way to deal with her, then hardball it is." Turning to Jean, he drew himself up from his casual slouch and said, "Tell Ms. Asher that I'll be waiting for her call."

Jean promised and busied herself discreetly as Katherine turned to go back to the elevators. She could hardly wait to get rid of John Wesley and slip back into her own skin—if she could.

Her nerves were stretched to the point of snapping, her muscles were trembling, she felt ready to explode. The switch had gone too far. He needed to be told the truth. Soon. Before his next visit to her office.

She pressed the Down button, then realized he hadn't followed her. She looked back. His gaze rose from her tush to her eyes. She went hot all over.

"You forgot to deliver your something personal," he said simply.

"Oh. Yes." She had a briefcase full of legal documents that wouldn't look very personal, so she reached into her purse and pulled out the first thing she touched.

She slapped a small packet of facial tissues down on Jean's desk.

"Will you see that my sister gets these, please?" Both of her companions looked mutely at the tissues. "She has a bad cold."

"A terrible cough too," Jean added. Katherine stared at her, her expression vapid.

Like a runaway train slipping off its track, Katherine suddenly started to dredge the bottom of her purse. She retrieved two paper-wrapped cough drops and set them beside the tissue. Tissue and cough drops—for a cold. She knew an unreal sense of satisfaction, as if she'd finally done something that made sense to her, that was in keeping with her fastidious character.

"You know," she said, functioning on impulse. "What I think I'll do is run these back to her office and leave them on her desk. That'll be better. And . . . and you don't need to wait for me, John, because I think I'll hang around and see how she's feeling when she gets back."

He was watching her with great interest, turning his body toward her so that he missed nothing.

"I . . . I haven't seen her in a couple of days and we're very close and she has been under the weather and all and . . ." She bottomed out mid-sentence. She couldn't tell one more lie. Couldn't pretend one more second. "I need time. Alone."

His smile was as gentle and understanding as it was proud and triumphant.

"Okay," he said, attributing her fluster to what he'd said in the elevator, thinking it adorable and delightful that she could be awkward and bashful and clearly unaccustomed to being so. He leaned forward to place a sweet, chaste kiss on her lips, then caressed her cheek lightly with the palm of his hand. "I'll be around."

Both women watched him saunter off, broad shouldered, tall, handsome, and confident. They waited for him to enter the elevator, then together released a wistful sigh.

FOUR

Two nights later, the twins, Andrea and Allison, were angelic in aqua tights and tutus, their dark hair bouncing with curls, cheeks flushed with excitement.

Quinn was reminding them, "Don't fight until you get off stage. That isn't what everyone's coming to see. And don't forget to bow at the end. Okay?"

Corrie, dressed too tightly in too little, was sitting on the bed in the master bedroom, putting a final coat of Ravish Me Red polish on her nails.

"Aunt Katherine, look at me. Aren't I pretty?" Andrea asked, spinning about so her aunt could see all of her.

"Lovely."

Allison walked quietly to her side and slipped an arm around her waist. "Are you coming to see me dance, Aunt Katherine?" she asked, a tiny thread of fear in her voice.

"How could I miss seeing two such beautiful and

talented young ballerinas perform?" she asked, giving Allison an encouraging squeeze. "And I have to tell you how proud I am of both of you for practicing your dance so well. Tonight will be easy, because you know the whole routine by heart. I bet you could do it in your sleep."

That was an interesting concept to the girls, who started twirling around with their eyes closed. But after the first couple of bumps and falls, their mother stepped in. "Please. Sit right here on the floor . . . oops, watch your little tutu, and look at these pictures. Remember this one? *The Nutcracker Suite*? We'll be ready to go soon."

"Go ahead. Say it," Corrie said to Katherine, not bothering to look up when she sat down on the bed beside her. "I've been ready to hear it all day."

"Remember our dance recital?" she asked, not wanting to disappoint her. "The one when you were so busy running around and bossing everybody else that you forgot to get nervous till the very last minute, and then you threw up on stage?"

Corrie sighed her relief, glad to have the memory out and over with. "We can't all be perfect."

"Who's perfect? I'm not perfect," Katherine stated with feeling. "Why do you two keep saying that?"

"Because you never do anything wrong," Quinn said, coming in on the conversation while she pulled up her pantyhose.

"But I do. All the time."

"No. You just think you do because you have an

overactive sense of guilt, and worry constantly about making mistakes that you'll have to feel guilty about later," Corrie said, blowing softly on her nails. "How many times did you have to stay after school when we were kids?"

"Never."

"I was in detention at least every other week. What about you, Quinn?"

"Oh, I think I was there the weeks you weren't," she said, looking up from a close examination of her shoes. "But . . . that was because they all thought I was you."

"Well, how come they never thought Katherine was me?" she asked, showing no remorse for mislaid blame in the past.

"Because I told them I wasn't you," she said. "So you see, it's not that I never make mistakes, it's that you make so many that Quinn feels she has to cover for half of them, and then by comparison it just looks as if I never make mistakes."

Her rationale struck both of them as funny at the same time, and they laughed together.

"Well, maybe so," Corrie said, "but you do have a strange way of making the kind of mistakes that turn out great." Katherine raised her brows. Her mistakes always felt like humdingers to her. "Such as kissing John Wesley the other night."

"You kissed John Wesley?" Quinn asked, shocked by Katherine's uncommon departure from the rules.

"It was an accident." The careless kind, but an accident nonetheless.

"How do you kiss someone by accident? Fall on their lips?"

"No. It just happens without you wanting it to." That was a lie. She'd wanted it to happen. "Without you meaning for it to happen."

Quinn tilted her head, taking a good long look at Katherine.

"Personally, I think it was meant to happen. Like fate," Corrie declared, seeming tickled to death about it. "He came in Monday morning and was as cocky and demanding as he usually is and I thought—no offense, Katherine—but I thought he'd forgotten all about the kiss. He spent the whole morning trying to tick me off over one thing and then another. But I kept my cool because, well, because I need the account. You'd have been proud of me. The next day he tried it again, going on and on about you canceling that appointment and how he had walking pneumonia one winter in Chicago and didn't miss a day of work with it—"

"But he couldn't have been nicer about that at the office," Katherine interjected, mystified. "He said rescheduling the appointment wouldn't be a problem."

"Well, I guess he'd had the time to think about it and work himself into a real snit, because I went home with a headache I thought I'd have for the rest of my life. I still had it this morning when he came by to meet with a couple of the mayor's men—we're combining our efforts with the mayor's reelection campaign to get as much milage as we can, by the way. . . . Anyway, he started up again, and I put my foot down right then and there. No account in the world is worth that kind of aggravation. So I asked him out into the hall."

"Oh no," her sisters chorused.

"Oh yes. I started a stink that would have put Saddam Hussein to shame." Her sisters stood bug-eyed before her. "Know what he did?" They shook their heads in unison. "He jerked my up off my feet and kissed me."

"He kissed you?" Quinn asked, while Katherine sat mute, a painful pressure building in her chest. "Then what happened?"

"My headache went away," she said, giggling. She shook a finger at Katherine. "You said he was a very nice kisser, not a fabulous kisser. I didn't think I'd ever be able to walk a straight line again. He said he'd been wondering how long it would take for him to get to me. And then he just walked back into the meeting."

"How did he act after that?" Quinn wanted to know.

"Like an honest-to-God human being. I mean, he was still difficult and demanding, but it was different. He was forceful without being obnoxious, you know? There was no more jabbing and cutting. And he winked at me twice during the meeting. Lord, I think I'm in love."

The light and joy in Katherine's life seemed to slowly seep away to darkness. In her mind she knew she had no right to feel disappointment or jealousy or betrayal, but in her heart she felt them all with acute clarity. She'd deluded herself into thinking that John could distinguish her from Corrie. She'd believed his kiss was something blessed and special for her alone. But he'd been kissing Corrie all along.

Robert joined them once Trevor was safely engrossed in a Bambi video with his babysitter, and they left for the recital. It went on as a sweet comedy of errors and triumphs that would have been heartwarming any other time. Katherine, however, felt cold and empty and closed off inside. She sat through two hours of enthusiastic tapping and graceless toe pointing, naming herself every sort of fool in the book.

It was virtually impossible to tell one sister from the other if one wasn't aware that there were three of them and looking for the subtle differences. It wasn't John's fault if he thought Corrie had more sides to her personality than a chameleon had colors. It served only to make her seem more fascinating. She couldn't blame Corrie for being attracted to John—who wouldn't be? Monday morning, hadn't Katherine insisted that she never wanted to hear or see John Wesley again? And hadn't she pressed the point that same afternoon after his visit to her office? There hadn't been any reason for Corrie not to believe her.

No, she was the fool who'd been in the wrong place at the wrong time as the wrong person. She was the fool who'd let a kiss—a kiss meant for someone else—go to her head . . . and her heart. She was the fool who had let her soul hope. And now she was the fool who would pay the price.

"Are you sure the two of you can't stay a little longer? The girls are so wired, it'll take at least four adults to get them to bed tonight," Quinn said, walking her sisters to the door after the postrecital party.

"You should have spiked their ice cream with Valium," Corrie said. "She never would admit to it, but I know Mom spiked ours more than once."

"She did not."

"Sure she did. How else can you explain the fact that we always fell asleep before we got to see Santa Claus and the Easter Bunny and the Tooth Fairy, huh?"

They dredged up childhood memories while inching their way toward the cars parked at the curb. Corrie was the first to call it a night, claiming another early appointment with John Wesley that would require plenty of rest to endure, and she drove off.

"Sometimes," Quinn said, soft and pensive, "if you have something on your mind, it's best to talk about it right away, rather than to let the problem slide and speak when it's too late to change anything."

"Where's this coming from? *Reader's Digest?*" Katherine asked, feeling invaded, as if her sister had crawled inside her soul and knew all her secrets.

"No," she said, reaching out impulsively to hug her. "It's coming from someone who knows you and loves you."

"Then tell her thanks, but I don't have anything

on my mind that she needs to worry about." Hoping to divert her mid-track, she changed scents and added, "I have a meeting with Belle Gumph tomorrow."

"The old lady who snaps at your heels?"

"And growls and barks—and everything else a mad dog might do, short of foaming at the mouth and chewing on the furniture." She opened the car door and got in. "When she finds out she's going to lose her buildings, she might actually draw blood this time."

"Is she going to lose them?"

Katherine nodded. "She's lost them. I met with a judge and their attorney this morning."

"John wasn't there?"

"No. He didn't need to be. It was just a formality, really. The city condemned the buildings, the judge ordered them vacated and set a selling price, then awarded the property to the city in eminent domain."

"What'll happen now?"

"Belle will fight it."

"And John Wesley?"

"I'll take care of John Wesley in court."

"Then it's time for John to meet Corrie's sisters."

"Maybe," she said, putting the keys in the ignition as she thought about it, not for the first time. "There's still a chance we can settle out of court. We'll see, huh?"

She smiled through the window at her sister, but the farewell on her lips faded when Quinn showed no signs of stepping away from the car to let her leave.

"What?" Katherine asked, tired of talking, tired of thinking, tired of pretending that she didn't want to curl up on her bed and close the world out with sleep.

"I was just thinking that John should meet us whether it goes to trial or not. Soon. So he'll know that he has a choice to make."

"What sort of choice?"

"Well, half of what he likes about Corrie is you. He should know that he's been dealing with more than one person, especially if . . . well, if he's going to keep kissing you both."

"He'll only be kissing Corrie from now on. If anything serious develops, it'll develop with her."

"But he kissed you first."

True, but he'd thought she was Corrie.

"It'll be easier on Corrie too," Quinn went on, "if John knows all the facts before she gets too wrapped up in him."

Or would his knowing destroy both their careers? Corrie's with the loss of his account and hers on ethics charges. . . . Or was she really worried about their careers? Wouldn't it be far worse for John Wesley to know all the facts, then consciously choose to kiss Corrie instead of her? She didn't want to think about it.

"If there's no trial, it'll be her decision," she said, starting the engine. "I'll talk to you tomorrow."

She drove home trying to keep her mind on the

meeting with Belle Gumph the next morning, but she kept seeing John and Corrie kissing. Her thoughts would turn black with emotions that turned to shame and regret in her heart.

She tried being pragmatic. *Que será será* and all that fatalistic mumbo jumbo that annoyed the hell out of her. She had a will. She had choices. Who said you had to sit back and take whatever life chose to give you? Hadn't fate handed her enough already? Sharing a face with two other people wasn't always a picnic. Why couldn't she fight Corrie for John?

No. That bubble popped before it was fully formed. Corrie was an infuriating flake with too much talent and not enough material in her clothes, who couldn't organize a deck of cards to save her life . . . but she was Katherine's sister. Born of the same ovum, nurtured by the same blood, the bond between the three Asher offspring went much deeper than flesh and emotion. It was anchored in their spirit, as if God had created all three of their souls of a single breath.

She pulled into the parking garage of her building and swung neatly into her parking space. She stood in front of the elevator for several minutes, lost in her thoughts, before she remembered to press the button. Her mind was a million miles away, contemplating life's idiosyncracies and other sundry cosmic forces—and it didn't return fast enough to enable her to do much more than gasp in utter shock when John Wesley stepped out of the elevator to greet her.

"Hi." He was almost as surprised as she was.

"Ah, Jeeze." Her whole body sagged in defeat. "What are you doing here?"

"Making your day," he said. A spark of hurt or maybe disappointment shown briefly in his eyes. "Or inspecting elevators. Take your pick."

All her coping mechanisms were thwarted. She wanted to sit on the floor and cry like a baby.

"My choice is that you were just leaving. Good night."

"Are you going to pretend you're not happy to see me?"

"I don't have to pretend."

"Are you angry that I tracked you down at your sister's?"

"My . . ." Lord, she'd forgotten! "What *are* you doing here?" she asked again, frustrated beyond belief that she had once again found herself in Corrie's place.

She was going to cry, she just knew she was going to cry. But no tears came, only the buildup of pressure in her throat, behind her eyes, and in her heart.

Unbelievably, he looked almost self-conscious and seemed unable to stop the hand that reached out to touch her lightly on the arm. He shook his head. "To tell you the truth, I'm not sure why I'm here. I . . . I wanted to see you. And the more I thought about it, the more I *needed* to see you."

"Is something wrong?" she asked, unable to resist the appeal of his vulnerability, unable to turn her back on his confusion.

"There's a lot wrong, but . . ." He took a deep breath and let it go. "Looking at you makes everything else seem unimportant somehow." He hesitated. "Look, I know you've come here to see your sister, but could we walk around the block or something first?"

"No. But I would like to know how you knew Katherine lived here?" she said, half grateful and half sorry that the masquerade wasn't over.

"It was in the phone book," he said, stepping away from the elevator doors, blocking her way in as they closed. "I called and talked to your machine once or twice, but they weren't very satisfying conversations, so I thought I'd drive over and wait for you to come home."

"That was pretty risky," she said, punching the Up button on the wall. "What if Michael had answered the phone? What if I'd come home with him?"

He turned his head and gave her a long, piercing look, then glanced away briefly, saying, "Actually, I did run into your friend while I was there. He was moving out."

"Oh," was all she could say. There were no more barriers, she realized. With Michael out of the picture, nothing stood between John and Corrie. The image was crushing.

"Why didn't you tell me?" he asked, a note of concern in his voice.

"It wasn't any of your business." He gave her a sharp look, but said nothing. "And you still haven't explained why you came *here*."

"If I wanted to avoid a lover who was moving out of my apartment, I'd hang out with a friend or my brother for a couple of hours. Since I don't know any of your friends or your married sister's last name, this was my only chance to see you tonight. It was a gamble that paid off."

It was a gamble that could have been disastrous. What if he'd come a half hour later and knocked on her door?

"What are you doing down here in the garage?" she asked.

"I was acting on an impulse, but I wasn't quite out of my mind. And I do have my pride, you know," he said. "I wasn't going up to your sister's place, get her out of her sick bed, and start whining to see you. I was going to wait for you to come out. But I couldn't spot your car on the street, so I came in to check in the garage."

"I see," she said thoughtfully. A familiar blackness swirled and churned inside her. "You've gone to a lot of trouble to see me tonight." To see Corrie. "Why do I have this feeling that you're not here to discuss flyers and posters?"

"Because you have good instincts," he said, smiling at her as he reached out to lock his fingers with hers.

The gesture was too sweet, too old-fashioned, and too intimate for Katherine. She shook her fingers free.

"You are angry," he said, his impression confirmed

and causing him more than a little uneasiness. "I guess I shouldn't have assumed that you'd want to see me too. I'm sorry."

She was angry. Very angry. Why couldn't he have gone to all that trouble to see *her*, instead of Corrie? How could he have kissed her sister?

She sighed heavily and let her gaze wander aimlessly about the garage, searching for an answer to the turmoil inside her.

How could she hold him accountable for kissing another woman when he had no idea who he was kissing in the first place, or the second place? Was kissing one woman so different from kissing another, if you thought the two women were the same person? Lord, it was too confusing.

"Don't be sorry," she said at last, resigned to the will of those asinine, ever-meddling fates she'd been thinking about earlier—moments before they'd forced another twist into her life. "I'm . . . flattered. Really. That you'd do all this, just to see me. I'm . . . a little out of sorts tonight."

This time his touch was so full of compassion and empathy, she couldn't reject him.

"Are you afraid he'll rob you blind?"

"Who?"

"That guy. Michael. Your ex-lover. If you think he might have sticky fingers, your new one can go back and keep an eye on him," he said sincerely.

"My . . . oh. No. I didn't know he was moving out tonight, but he's welcome to anything he wants, so long as he's gone by the time I get back," she said, speaking purely for Corrie. "By my new one, I suppose you mean that you think you're going to be my new lover, huh?"

"I know I am," he said, as if it were written in stone somewhere.

She laughed as the elevator doors opened, forgetting for an instant who she was—and who he thought he was talking to.

"Some women don't like cocky, arrogant men, you know," she said, warming to those same qualities in him because she'd also seen him self-conscious and doubtful, kind and thoughtful.

"I'm only interested in what you like."

"And you think it's cocky, arrogant men?"

"I think it's this cocky, arrogant man."

Again she laughed, but she couldn't deny his assumption. She did like him. She liked him very much, but if she had to explain why, it would be difficult to put into words. It had a lot to do with the way he looked at her. She knew it was crazy, that it couldn't be true, but . . . well, she still had the feeling that he knew her—her, Katherine—despite the fact that he thought she was Corrie. Oh, she knew how weird that sounded. It made no sense at all. But somehow she thought that if there were a hundred women with her face, he'd be able to pick her out of the crowd. Truly.

She gave herself a mental shake. He'd kissed Corrie and couldn't tell the difference.

"Well, now that you've seen me . . ." she said, thinking it best to keep any further contact with him to a minimum—for everyone's sake. "Did you want to see me about something specific, or did you just need to bask in my beauty before you could get a good night's sleep?"

"Looking at you doesn't exactly make me sleepy," he said, doing so with a lazy, seductive warmth in his eyes. "And I did want to talk to you about that kiss at the office today."

"What about it?" She spoke so quickly and harshly that she startled him.

The electric doors kept trying to close, so she stepped in front of them. He reached inside to press the Hold button, took her by the shoulders, and turned her toward him, demanding her full attention. "We need to talk. Now. Tonight. It's important. Do you think you could call your sister and cancel your plans? Have a cup of coffee with me instead?"

"Do you know how late it is?"

"If coffee keeps you awake, we'll get warm milk, water . . . but we have to talk."

"About the kiss?"

"About the kiss, you and me, other things. I . . . it's important."

She could see that he thought it was important. But the last thing in the world she wanted to discuss with him was the kiss he'd shared with Corrie, or the two of them, or other things that involved *them*.

"Couldn't you tell me here? I don't think I'm going to like what you have to say."

"No. I can't tell you here. I want to go somewhere private and quiet . . . and far away, so you can't get up and run away from me again."

"I don't run away."

"Not at the office maybe, but when we're alone, when it's personal, you do."

"I don't," she said, aware for the first time that he hadn't been with Corrie socially yet, only at the office. "I mean, I'm not really running away from you, it's just that I think it best not to start something we can't finish or that we'll finish in a disaster."

"How do you know it'll be a disaster?"

"Trust me."

"Trust what you say?" he asked, moving closer. "Or trust what I see in your eyes and feel in your kiss?"

"Oh, please. There's nothing in my eyes that a few hours of sleep won't cure. If you see anything else, it's your imagination." Suddenly everything about her seemed out of place. She looked around as if shaken from a dream. "Just tell me what it is you came to say."

"Don't kiss me anymore."

"What?"

"Don't kiss me at work anymore, okay?" It was her stunned expression that had him speaking again, swiftly. "I can't concentrate on anything. I think about you constantly. Things you've told me. Kissing you. Touching you. How soon I can get you alone again.

It's driving me crazy. And kissing at work only makes it worse."

"Well, excuse me," she said, hurt and indignant, even though she hadn't been—or maybe *because* she hadn't been—the one he'd been kissing at work. "But it seems to me that it takes two to tango, and two to kiss."

"It does. You're right and . . . and that kiss today was great but, well, let's not kiss during the day . . . during work hours. Okay?"

"Get away from me," she said, angry. She stepped into the elevator and released the Hold button. "If you don't want to kiss me, then keep your lips to yourself."

He slipped inside the elevator with her before the doors closed and palmed the Hold button once again.

"That's the problem," he said, standing close, his mouth inches from hers. "I can't keep my lips to myself. Kissing you is all I can think about. That's all I want to do, all day, all night." He supped gently on her lower lip.

She opened her mouth to protest, but nothing came out. Instead, he moved in, his tongue sweeping deep to remove any words that might stop him, any sound that might call to mind an element of sanity or reason.

He pressed her to the wall, and her body took his weight greedily. The earth tilted on its axis, and the sun and the stars slipped from their natural orbits.

Hands wandered and clutched. Life breath and emotions mingled. Katherine grew weak in his arms.

"This can't be happening," she muttered, her mind spinning off in all directions. "Not now. Not with you."

"Why? Because of that guy? Because you've just ended a relationship?" He was doing the most incredible things with his mouth at the base of her neck. "They say that when you fall off a horse . . . hmm . . . you like that?"

"Yes. No. Yes. Please stop. I need to think."

"You think too much."

"I do, don't I?" She sighed and allowed his touch to overwhelm her. "Everybody thinks I think too much."

"What else does everybody think about you?" he asked, loosening a few of the buttons on her blouse.

"I'm too careful, too cautious," her head fell back to rest against the elevator wall, "too afraid to risk anything. Aw-um. Oh my. They . . . they say I never make mistakes. I'm perfect."

"Damn close, I'd say," he murmured, agreeing with the perfect part, hoping the rest wasn't true. The skin at the base of her neck was warm and sweet; the pulse in her throat hammered against his lips, baiting him, luring him, tempting him to seek out the soft, shadowy places closer to its source.

He parted the front of her blouse, peeling it blindly from her shoulders. He pressed his need to the forward thrust of her pelvis, bending low to taste the soft swell of her breasts above the sculptured black lace bra.

Her skin was warm and smooth, softer than his own lips. The gentle moans from her throat hummed in his ears. His heart raced and his body quickened.

She locked her knees to keep from sliding to the floor. It felt too good to stretch her body the length of his, to press inch to inch, nose to toes. It was too right to feel his heart beating close to hers, to feel his arms about her, strong and secure. It was too wonderful to be whole and free at once, to have her head in the clouds and her body feeling earthy, carnal, sensuous.

He cupped her breasts with both hands; his mouth left hers gasping for air.

She let out a sound that was half startled scream and half groan of misery, when the elevator alarm pierced the air.

"No. No." Her hands pushed against his chest when he would have ignored the shrill alarm to feed his passion at her breast. "John. No. This isn't right," she said, her throat tight, her words a bare whisper.

He recoiled as if she'd slapped him or cried out another man's name. Then, as the emotion in his eyes cleared, he shook his head.

"Corrie, we have to talk," he bellowed over the noise. "I can't go on like this. There are things I need to tell you. Things I want to say to you."

She was nodding helplessly, still too weak to speak, her hands twisted in his shirtfront.

"Yes. Yes."

The elevator alarm shrieked on while he hastily helped her button her blouse. "Now. Can we go somewhere now and talk? I want everything settled between us. No secrets. No old boyfriends. No more tricks. No more running away. Just you and me. Alone. Just to talk. That's all."

"Yes. We do have to talk, but . . . but not tonight. There are things I have to take care of first and then we'll talk. I promise. I . . . I need to tell you something important too. And . . . and I want to tell you, but I can't yet. Saturday," she said decisively. "Saturday afternoon, I'll meet you for lunch at Anton's, where we had dinner that first night. I'll meet you there and we'll talk. Okay?"

It wasn't at all okay. Saturday was a lifetime away. A whole day. But she seemed adamant about waiting, and he was too glad that she saw the necessity for them to talk to quibble. He was about to capitulate when a thought struck him.

"We won't be meeting again between now and then, will we?"

"You mean at the office?"

He nodded.

"Tomorrow morning?"

He frowned. "No kissing," he said. "Promise you won't kiss me again until Saturday."

"I promise, if you will," she said, as if the bargain made pure and perfect sense.

He silenced the alarm and rode the elevator up to the lobby.

"Saturday at Anton's. Twelve noon. Right?" he asked, holding the door.

"Right."

He shifted his body to deliver her a swift kiss and stood aside with his hands in his pockets as the door closed between them.

FIVE

"We can go to court if you want, Belle," Katherine said early the next morning. "We have a couple of good arguments we can plea. But I have to be honest with you, we'll probably lose."

"Young lady, I don't like your attitude," Belle Gumph said, getting to her feet. She was all of five feet two in three-inch heels, thin and spry. When she spoke, it was as if she had a high-fidelity megaphone stuck in her throat. "Do you know where I'd be today if me and my Darwood, God love him, had gone around saying we were going to lose before we even tried to win?"

"You pay me to be realistic, Belle."

"All right, I'll tell you where I'd be today," she went on. Belle also claimed to be hearing impaired, though Katherine suspected it was more a convenience than a handicap. "I'd be down in one of those buildings, packing up to move out into the streets, wondering how long I'd last as a bag lady."

Katherine said nothing. Experience told her that she was about to be taught a lesson from the annals of Belle Gumph's life. She wouldn't be expected to mutter more than a few monosyllables until it was over.

She glanced despondently at the phone. She hadn't been able to get through to Corrie, and it was almost noon. Was she still with John? Breakfast meetings were for breakfast, for crying out loud. What were they doing? Laying their own eggs? She was brooding over several other activities they might be involved in when she realized that Belle was asking her a question.

"I bet you think that I was always a rich old broad who had nothing better to do than to count her money and pester her lawyer."

"No. I . . . no."

"You never thought of me as being young once, did you?"

"No. I guess not."

"I was," she said, walking to the window, staring out at the horizon. "I never was a looker, but I was smart and I could work hard. And Darwood, God love him, was even uglier than me. Nothing to scream about, that's for sure. But he was a good man. Kind. Even sweet sometimes. And clever as hell when it came to money."

She chuckled softly, and Katherine turned in her chair to watch her as she continued to speak.

"We grew up down there on the river, in those buildings. Me in one and Darwood in the other. That was our neighborhood. We'd walk past those dark warehouses on our way to school. We'd sit on each other's stoop and dream and make plans . . . and we'd neck."

"Neck?" Katherine asked, startled.

"Kiss. Don't young people neck anymore?" she asked, glancing over her shoulder.

"Oh. Sure. Yes, they neck." She was trying to recall if she'd discussed necking with any of her clients before.

Belle nodded and turned back to the window.

"Darwood wasn't what you'd call a thrill a minute, but he sure could kiss," she said, her voice wistful.

"Is that why you want to keep those buildings, Belle? Because you and Darwood grew up there?"

"And fell in love there. And got married there. And moved away from there to build a better life for ourselves," she said. She walked back to the chair and sat very straight, a little taller than before. "As you well know, I'm not a sentimental person. Not as a rule. But I have no children and I've outlived everyone I've ever cared about. All I have left are my memories, those two old buildings, and more money than I know what to do with. I intend to use the one to save the others. And if you can't show me the proper attitude, missy, I'm afraid I won't be able to let you help me."

Katherine couldn't help smiling.

"I'm glad we had this talk, Belle," she said, liking the old woman in spite of herself. "There's nothing I like better than a good fight with a windmill."

Belle nodded sagely and let loose a rare smile of her own. "I knew that about you the minute I saw you. It's in your eyes."

Her eyes again. Perhaps she should start wearing dark glasses, she mused.

"You need to know something else about this case, Belle," she said, her ethics compromised, her guilt riding high in her mind. "My sister is working for the Wesley brothers. She has a public relations firm and is handling their press and advertising."

"So?"

"So ethically I'm bound to tell you, and you're free to obtain another lawyer's services if you think there's a conflict of interest on my part."

"Is there?"

"No. Not where my sister's concerned, but you should know, too, that I've met John Wesley on several occasions socially."

Belle smiled. "He's a cute little bugger, isn't he? If I were forty years younger, I'd be seeing him privately, if you know what I mean." She cackled licentiously.

Katherine wanted to close her eyes to keep Belle from reading her thoughts—and because the picture of John with Belle Gumph was . . . well, it wasn't funny, but it made her want to laugh anyway. It was all she could do to nod in agreement.

Belle cocked her head and said, "Actually, I would have thought the other one, Peter, would have suited you better. John, he's full of piss and vinegar all right, but the other one . . . He's the one you want to watch out for. He's the brains behind the operation. Real smart."

"I haven't met Peter."

"Then you're in for a treat, young lady. Two handsome fellas sitting side by side like bookends, pretty near took my breath away. Course, they're different as diamonds and rubies, but still, they're a sight to see."

"Yes, well, the point I'm trying to make here is that—"

"I know the point," Belle interrupted sternly, miffed that her own attorney didn't seem to be heeding her romantic advice. "The point is, who are *you* working for?"

"You," she said without hesitation.

"Then the matter is settled."

"Stop looking at me like that," Corrie said later that afternoon, her arms folded defensively in front of her. "If it'll make you feel any better, we didn't do all that much kissing. We pretty much went straight for the floor." A pause. "Lord, we were like animals," she added, as amazed as she was defiant.

"Oh, Corrie." Quinn moaned miserably, positioned once again between her sisters, seeing both sides objectively, sympathetic toward both.

"The day before yesterday you hated him," Katherine said, her voice low, angry, and accusing. "What were you thinking? You get one kiss in a hallway, and the next time you see him, you throw him to the floor and have sex?"

"Katherine," Quinn cautioned her.

"What do you know about him?" Katherine went on. "Have you spent any time with him socially? No. Have you talked about his life beyond the river project? No. Do you know how he feels about his work, his life, what his hopes are? No."

"I know enough," Corrie said, feeling as hurt and abused as her sister. "I like him. He likes me. We're both direct. We're both aggressive. We both like to get to the point. That's all I need to know."

"How romantic. Did you tell him to take off his pants before or after you invited him into your apartment?"

"I told you what happened," Corrie said. "He woke me up at two in the morning. I was half asleep. He said he couldn't sleep because he was worried about me being in the apartment alone after Michael left, and did I want someone to talk to? I couldn't very well slam the door in his face and go back to bed, so I invited him in. We . . . talked . . . and one thing led to another and . . ."

Katherine was heartsick. She pushed her hair back from her face with both hands and blew out a long, dejected sigh, her shoulders slumping low.

"I didn't know you were falling for him too," Corrie said. "You could have told me."

"I didn't think I'd need to at first. It was a switch. I couldn't act on my own feelings because I was supposed to be you and you had Michael and you didn't care much for John. And then there was the second switch, and it seemed like every time I turned around, he was there thinking I was you." She blinked her eyes hard to keep from crying. "Every time I saw him, I thought it would be for the last time, and he was your important client and . . ."

She glanced at Quinn and then over at Corrie, making a small smile with a giant effort. "I didn't know until last night, when he came for you at my apartment, how much I wanted a next time or how much I needed him to know who I really am. I couldn't just blurt it out. And I thought I should check with you before I said anything. I thought we could work it out. The three of us. I didn't know how you really felt about him either and . . ." her eyes lowered to the floor in a twinge of guilt, "I know you wouldn't have . . . have, you know . . . I mean, I realize now that you have feelings for him too. But I didn't last night. And I didn't know your breakfast meeting with him would start at two in the morning. I thought we'd have time to talk."

There didn't seem to be anything else to say. It was like the ultimate irony designed by the Consummate Switch Master, that the two sisters would fall in love with the unknowing victim of their childish prank.

Quinn's kitchen was so quiet, they soon found themselves listening for and anticipating the next drip from the leaky faucet.

"What are we going to do now?" Quinn asked

at last, voicing the question on everyone's mind.

"Nothing," Katherine said with a determined edge to her voice. "We'll all go to Anton's tomorrow as planned, and John can meet Corrie's sisters. We won't mention the switch."

"Oh no," Corrie protested, springing to her feet. "You're not going to get to play the martyr for the rest of your life over this. I think we should tell him about the switch so he can choose me fair and square."

"What if he's furious and fires you? What if he decides he wants me?"

Corrie frowned. The John she knew had a short fuse on his temper, but in the eye of his stormy emotions was a vast calm of gentleness and understanding. She didn't doubt that John would forgive her, eventually. But it could also mean the end of her business if John was angry enough to go public with their duplicity.

After some thought, Quinn offered a solution. "We could not tell him about the switch, and neither sister could get further involved with him. That would be fair."

Katherine and Corrie exchanged glances. Without words, they agreed that neither of them was willing to give him up and shook their heads.

"Then we'll have to tell him the whole story and take our chances," Quinn deduced, hoping with all her might that John was a kind and wise man. One who might laugh at their stupidity. One who couldn't choose one sister over the other.

❖━━━━━━━❖

Anton's seemed a fitting place to meet. A crowded restaurant was, of course, the last place one would want to have to tell a man that he'd been wooing two different women, that he'd been tricked and lied to on more than one occasion. If he chose to pitch a fit or tried to strangle one or more of them, it would be fitting, part of the definitive payback, that the audience would be packed to standing room only.

And who would be the one to tell him? They drew straws.

"I'll go in first," the loser said, her heart hammering. "If we go together, he'll go through the roof. Five minutes, then you come in and get your share of all this. Agreed?" It was. "Five minutes. Not a second longer."

Katherine's first step was the hardest, but as Corrie pushed her from behind, it was over and done with before she could change her mind. After that, her feet moved automatically, stopping in front of the maitre d', then stepping unrelentingly toward John Wesley's table.

She cringed as she took note of John's preparations. He was obviously expecting to have an intimate lunch with Corrie, as he'd taken a secluded booth, sheltered from the rest of the restaurant by a lattice and clinging vines.

She forced a smile to her lips and felt it sag as she rounded the barrier.

Two! There were two of them! Two Johns! No.
One John and an identical twin. No. Not identical—
well, physically they were, but the twin . . . she recognized the twin. He was the one she'd met coming out
of the elevator from Corrie's office. The sharp, all-
business, get-to-it one who'd thought she'd forgotten
their appointment.

Her eyes narrowed as she looked from brother
to brother. They couldn't have been more different.
They were like two sides of the same coin, black and
white, a gusty wind and a gentle breeze, a go-getter
and a just-get-it-done guy.

"Corrie, I know what you're thinking," the gentle
breeze, just-get-it-done side of the coin said. He got
up to stand beside her. He took her hand as if he were
afraid she'd bolt and pressed his other soothingly to her
back as she stood staring in stunned disbelief. "Please,
just give me a chance to explain this."

When she didn't speak or try to run off, he guided
her carefully into the booth between him and his
brother.

"Peter . . ." the twin said.

"No. You just keep quiet now. I told you I'd explain
it to her, and then you'd get your chance to talk," he
said, the tension between them as strong and fierce as
that between her and Corrie.

"You're Peter?" she asked, amazed that she could
speak at all.

He nodded his admission slowly. "I know what you
must be feeling right now, but I swear I didn't mean

for this to hurt you in any way. I . . . Damn. I practiced this over and over, and now I don't know what to say. I . . . what I did was inexcusable. It was childish. It was stupid and dumb and I'm really sorry."

He was sorry? She felt as if she'd walked through a mirror backward. Everything was upside down and inside out. She wanted to laugh hysterically. But he was too sincere, too wretched, too . . . too much Peter, to be laughed at.

Beside her John took her hand under the table and gave it a gentle squeeze. She looked at him. There in his eyes was the laughter that gurgled in her heart. He knew. He knew she wasn't Corrie and was terribly amused that his brother didn't.

"Dammit, will you stop that?" Peter snapped suddenly, reaching across her lap to disentangle her fingers from his brother's. "She's too confused as it is. You've already slept with her. Now she needs to know that she slept with the wrong guy."

"Peter, I—" she started, then stopped when she felt John's elbow in her ribs.

"Corrie, sweetheart, I know how weird this must be for you, and I swear I didn't mean for this to happen. I met with you that first night, here at Anton's, because John hated you . . . well, you'd rubbed him wrong, is all. But he was going to stand you up to teach you a lesson. So I came instead, to see if you were really as bitchy as he said you were, and to try and smooth things over between the two of you for the sake of the project." He paused. "That happens sometimes. I mean, some people get along better with me than with John, and sometimes it's the other way around. Once you get to know us, you'll see that we're very different people. The thing is, I . . . I'm not . . . I don't . . ."

"He's trying to tell you that he doesn't fall in love with every woman that comes his way," John stated pragmatically, leaning forward. "He's been saving his heart for an angel in white flowing gowns, and, in case you've missed the resemblance, he thinks that's you."

"Shut up, John." Peter touched her chin and brought her gaze back to meet his. "When you came back that night, from the ladies' room? It was as if . . . I don't know, it was as if I hadn't been with you all that night. It was as if I was seeing you for the first time. There was something about you, in your eyes, in the way you moved your hands and tilted your head and . . . Lord, I don't know. It sounds crazy, doesn't it? But that's when I fell in love with you, at that moment, with crème brulée on your lower lip and—" he stopped, his eyes scanning her face and hair as if he worshipped every pore and follicle, "the light in your eyes."

"Peter, I—" she began once again, this time to have him silence her with a finger to her lips.

"Please, let me finish," he asked softly. "I didn't tell John that I was still seeing you after that first night. And I didn't know his feelings toward you were changing until he told me that he'd kissed you at the office and that he was planning to pursue you. And . . .

well, by then I was hopelessly in love, and I wasn't sure what to do. So I went looking for you, to get you to stop kissing John until I could figure out what to do about him. I wanted to tell you about me. And then, well, we got a little sidetracked." He shook his head with regret. "I didn't know he'd been to your place after I was there that night. He ran into that guy, Michael, like I did, and he was worried about you. I thought I'd have time to talk to him before he left for work the next morning, but . . ." his eyes shifted away uncomfortably. His distress was acute, a palpable thing that tore at Katherine's heart. "Look, I know that the two of you shared something special and all that." He sighed heavily. "And I don't have any right to ask anything of you, after the way I deceived you. But now that you know the truth and if you don't think it's too late, I'd like a chance. I want you to know me, as me."

"Peter, I'm so sorry," she said, wishing she'd made her own confession days earlier to save him the misery of his.

"So, you can't forgive me," he said, misconstruing her words.

"No. It's not that."

"You can forgive me, but you're in love with John."

"No. That's not it either."

"You mean you don't love John? It was just sex?" He was appalled. His angel was growing horns and a tail, or so it seemed from his expression. "You don't love either of us, but you had sex with John because

I got you hot in the elevator? What kind of a woman are you?"

John, who'd been listening with his chin on his fist, let his fist fall to the table in an act of total boredom.

"She's the kind of woman who has a secret of her own, brother."

"What?"

"This isn't the woman I slept with."

"What?"

"This isn't Corrie Asher."

Peter looked at her and then back to his poor demented brother.

"This is the woman I love, John. I'd know her anywhere."

"Maybe. But she's not Corrie Asher."

"Then who the hell is she?"

"She's my sister Katherine," Corrie said, rounding the partition, Quinn on her heels.

They were as surprised to see two John Wesleys as Katherine had been, but they recovered in half the time, smiling identical smiles while Peter stared on with saucer eyes and John let loose a hoot of amusement.

"Three of them," he said, laughing. "It's better than I thought. We're a full house." He enjoyed his poker-hand analogy all alone, then reached out and took Corrie's hand, pulling her into the booth beside him. "This one's mine. This one's Corrie."

"And I'm Quinn," the last sister said, feeling like

the fifth wheel. Taking the only space available, she slid into the booth beside Peter. "I belong to Robert, my husband."

The picture developed slowly in Peter's mind.

"Corrie," he muttered, acknowledging the fact that he hadn't met her before. "Quinn," he said, recognizing the warm friendliness about her. They'd eaten dinner together. She'd gone off to the ladies' room and . . .

He turned his head to look at Katherine. Katherine. A rose by any other name, he thought, and he would have loved her just the same.

"You're mine?" he asked. His query wasn't presumptive. It wasn't possessive. It was a simple question with a hundred answers, each as important as the next.

She nodded, and in her eyes he saw the passion that had attracted him first; knew the longing and isolation that had touched his own; perceived the strength and intelligence he admired in her; understood parts of her that had confused him before. He remembered her willingness to give, her sweetness, the feel of her in his arms. He knew her, even before she said the words, "I'm Katherine."

SIX

"So," he said.

"So," she returned, her hands moving out from her sides in a gesture of readiness.

There hadn't been any question to their leaving Anton's together. His hotel suite was closer than her apartment, so they hadn't questioned going there either. What now? was the burning question between them. What now and how soon can I touch you?

The confrontation was over, the lies they'd hidden behind were gone. Though nothing had changed between them, things in general were different. They were Katherine and Peter now, and they were like intimate strangers. It was almost as if they were starting over—but not.

"Ripping our clothes off and falling on each other is always a good ice breaker," he said from across the room, looking hopeful.

"You know this for a fact, do you?" she said with raised brows. She felt as if a flock of swallows had taken flight in her midsection.

Discretion and valor being what they were, however, he smiled and said, "Wishful thinking. I suppose we should talk."

She was much more inclined toward his first suggestion and was eager to start ripping, but . . .

She nodded. "I expected you to go through the ceiling at the restaurant. If you feel like you still might want to, it's okay. You have every right to," she said, feeling guilty for what she'd done.

Somehow it was worse to have transgressed and gotten away with it than to have sinned and done a proper penance.

He tilted his head and studied her. "You're big on rights, aren't you?" She looked confused. "Come over here," he said, sitting on the couch, making a place for her to join him. "This is a good place for us to start."

"Start what?"

"Filling in the gaps. My being an architect wasn't part of my lie," he said, scooting closer to her, easing his need to touch her by taking her hand. "Your being a lawyer wasn't something I'd bargained on."

"And you're not fond of lawyers, are you?" she asked, accustomed to being in an unpopular profession.

"Not in general, no. But that doesn't mean I haven't fallen in love with one."

"But you want to know what kind of an attorney I am."

"You're hardworking and fair. I checked that out, remember? I think I'd rather know why."

"Why I chose law?" He nodded, studying her face. She laughed softly and looked away. "I wonder about that myself sometimes. I know what first appealed to me."

"Human rights."

"*Individual* human rights," she corrected. "Being an individual was stressed at our house. My parents downplayed our likenesses and encouraged us to be who we thought we were. They were also big on being totally fair with us. If one got something, so did the other two, that sort of thing. Likewise, if one of us wanted something special and they couldn't get something of like value for the others, we'd have to do without."

"And what didn't you get?" he asked, wishing he'd known her as a little girl.

"No, it wasn't me. It was Quinn."

"Quinn?"

Quinn had felt cheated, so Katherine took up law? He gave her a lost look, and she laughed.

"Quinn loved music. Corrie and I like it, too, but we didn't have the burning desire to play anything musical. Not like Quinn. So when Quinn wanted to play the piano and we didn't, she couldn't have lessons until we found something of an equal value that we wanted to do. Corrie had sports. So when Quinn played the piano, Corrie played soccer. And when Quinn wanted to take up the flute as well, Corrie played basketball and then tennis."

"And what did Katherine like to do?" he asked.

"Oh, she liked to read," she said, knowing how boring it sounded. "She liked to walk in the woods around her house and go down to the river and lie on the bottom of the boat and watch the clouds pass over. Real exciting things like that, expensive things like that."

"And she felt left out?"

"No, she used to wish that she could be left out," she said. He shook his head, disoriented once again, so she continued. "In order for the other two to have what they wanted, I suffered piano lessons, to discover that I was tone-deaf; basketball, swimming, soccer, tennis, golf, and karate lessons, to find out that I wasn't athletic; art classes, to be told that I couldn't draw a straight line . . . and dance, of course."

"So, you can dance," he said, one arm bent over the back of the couch, his fingers playing with her hair.

"Oh yeah. Just like those elephants you see at the circus."

"Then poor dull, bookish, and untalented Katherine turned to the study of law?" He shook his head. "I don't see the connection."

"That's because I never was poor or dull or untalented," she said in earnest. And there it was, that inner light that flared in her eyes whenever her emotions flared. "I traveled all over the world before I learned how to drive. I read volumes on Tibet, China, Russia, Portugal, Spain, Greece. I knew all about the San Andreas fault, the Shawnees and the Seminoles, the Rosenbergs, the Trojan War, the Amazon River. I knew about chromosomes and the collective unconscious and coral reefs. Stuff that no one else cared about"—she slapped her chest—"I knew about. I read and reread Steinbeck and Hemingway; I fell in love with Sancho Panza when I was twelve."

"Who?"

"Sancho Panza. Don Quixote's ever faithful squire."

"Why?"

"That's another story." She grinned.

"Tell me."

"I think I identified with him," she said, feeling a little silly. She shrugged. "I was always pretty sure that my sisters were a little bit nuts. They were always boy crazy and—"

"And you weren't."

"No. Not when I was twelve. But they were my sisters and I was faithful and loyal to them, even in their craziness."

He chuckled. He was feeling a little crazy himself. He was drawn to her like a flower to sunlight. He wanted to tap into the energy she exuded from within, feed off her passion.

" 'Faithful' and 'loyal' aren't words that automatically bring lawyers to mind, you know," he said, his fingers teasing the back of her neck.

"I know. But they bring Sancho to mine." She smiled. He couldn't keep his hand still in hers. He was tracing, rubbing, stroking, shooting shivers up her arm. She curbed the urge to shake her hand free. It was an exercise in mind over stimuli to continue. "Those same words remind me that I did a lot of things I didn't want to do because I loved my sisters. My view of fair and equal treatment is different from other people's. I think it's just as important to leave people alone as it is to include them. Even as a kid I knew that what was right for some, wasn't for others, and that no one rule could apply—or should apply—to everyone."

"Ah, the human rights issue." His fingers left hers to lie loosely across her knee.

"Individual human rights," she corrected, her fingers idly playing with a button halfway up the front of his shirt.

"Okay. So, how come you're not a public defender or some sort of altruistic crusader for kids who are forced to take dance classes?"

"I thought about it," she said, trying to hide her surprise when the button suddenly slipped loose of its hole. "But my parents were equally diligent in spoiling all their children. They helped us through college, but we were on our own during graduate school. I hadn't finished my first year of law school before I came to the conclusion that I hated being poor." She giggled. "It was a terrible revelation about myself, and I still get a little depressed over it, but then I go shopping and it passes."

He laughed, but he sensed there was more—he knew there was more. She could make herself sound complaisant and self-indulgent, but hell, she'd fallen in love with fat, dumpy, loyal little Sancho Panza when she was twelve . . . he knew better.

"Dempsey and Evens is a good firm," he said casually, his hand moving over her silk-covered knee. "Big money. They can have their pick of law school litters."

She grinned, and the light that never failed to stir him shone in her eyes.

"Actually, I picked them," she said with no little amount of pride. "I was seventh in my class at Yale and had my choice between two firms here, one in New York, and three in Chicago."

He couldn't stand it anymore. The glow in her eyes was like a bright blue tractor beam, pulling him in. He kissed her hard, fisting her hair in one hand while the other shot up her skirt like a heat-seeking missile. The thought that he might be rushing her did flicker through his mind, but flicker was about all it did before he felt her hands inside his shirt.

"Let me guess," he said, freeing his mouth abruptly, his words breathy as he reached for the short, tailored jacket she wore over her dress. "You picked Dempsey and Evens to be close to your sisters."

"Partly," she said, fumbling with the rest of his buttons, his tie, and sport jacket all at once. "But I almost went to New York."

"But Dempsy and Evens had a higher percentage

of pro bono cases," he said as if he'd read it somewhere. "And now you do most of them."

She looked startled. "How did you know?"

"I know you," he said, his words coming out gruff as he wrestled with the zipper on her dress. When it opened, he smiled and slowed his movements a bit to say it again.

"I know you," he said softly, like a tender caress.

He did know her, she thought, as she touched his cheek. It was a little beard-stubbled and rough against her palm, and it struck her as odd that a face so full of love and gentleness would feel coarse to the touch. The sureness of his hands and the intense passion that lurked in his eyes were a challenge she could meet, looked forward to meeting.

Her pulse was racing and she was trembling. He leaned close and kissed her, and she felt as if things inside her were shattering. Old things. Secret things. Things ever fresh but long forgotten. Hurts and doubts.

He brought his knees to the couch and deepened the kiss, pulling the bodice of her dress from her shoulders, then the thin silk straps of her bra.

Her mind reeled with senseless thoughts and inspiring sensations. Her hands grappled with his belt buckle. His lips to her breast were like fire to dynamite, hot and exploding.

Then suddenly she was in his arms, being lifted high up off the couch. She opened her eyes and looked directly into his, saw the inferno of his desires and trembled with trepidation.

"No room on that couch," he muttered hoarsely before he headed blindly toward the bedroom.

He bonked her head on the doorjamb going through it.

"Jeez." He started to laugh. "I'm sorry. Are you okay?"

She nodded and rubbed her pain as he laid her gently on the bed, sitting on the edge beside her. He took a deep breath and let it loose.

"I feel as if it's my first time up to bat. I'm like a kid with this beautiful girl, running for home base," he said, amused. "Only I wasn't this nervous the first time. I've made love to you a hundred times in my head, and it was always slow and thorough. One night I fell asleep, it took so long."

They laughed. Their gazes caught. In that moment, silent vows of trust and understanding were exchanged. In that moment, they knew their lives were about to be irreversibly altered, and they accepted that change, good or bad. In that moment, something far greater than what they understood to be love bound them together forever.

His hand, almost reverent in its touch, settled warm and gentle on her bare chest.

"I love you," he said simply and sincerely, vaguely amazed that words long avoided and rarely spoken could come so easily to his lips.

She laid a hand over his, stretching the other out to guide his face closer to hers.

Music played softly, a soft stringy instrumental that Katherine recognized. Quinn would know the name and history of it, she thought, also thinking it strange—the things one thought about when one wasn't really thinking at all.

"Have you ever given much thought to the concept of a parallel existence?" Peter asked suddenly, his arms folded beneath his head as he stared up at the ceiling from his bed.

Katherine didn't move a muscle. Peter had given "love in the afternoon" new meaning in the past few hours. All she could manage, as she lay with her head on his chest and one leg sprawled carelessly over his, was a concerted effort to keep her breathing even and deep, and a weary prayer that he'd think she'd fallen asleep.

Truth was, she was too happy to sleep, or maybe she was too happy and afraid to sleep for fear that when she woke, she'd find it was all a dream.

Hadn't the day's events been a little too easy? she kept wondering. Instead of the anger and rage she'd expected to encounter at the restaurant, she'd found love. The five of them had laughed and eaten a festive meal together. They'd even exchanged pecks on the cheek before heading off in three directions. It was so simple. It felt so right. Maybe it was too simple.

Too right. Too much like a dream come true. Was it any wonder that she was afraid to close her eyes?

Either way, she was awake and very aware that Peter was ready to embark on another mind-shattering, sensor-teasing, muscle-quaking journey to bliss . . . and she felt like a limp slab of bread dough.

"Actually, I don't think a parallel existence is possible," he went on, content for the moment with the sound of his own voice. "If you think about it, it's bad enough just knowing that somewhere in this town, my twin brother is making love to your identical sister. If we all had parallel counterparts somewhere, that would make four of us—eight altogether. That would be . . . quads. Quads making love to quads. And if we all did it at four in the afternoon, which is just four minutes from now, by the way, it would be . . . four into four at four . . . in four."

She didn't laugh aloud, but her stomach muscles spasmed in her effort to hold it inside.

"Thinking about it boggles my mind," he said. She thought his mind was boggled to consider it in the first place. "And the chances of it being possible would have to be . . . quadstronomical."

A giggle slipped through in the form of a snort.

"Katherine?" he whispered after several moments of peaceful quiet, his voice soft and tender, too sweet for her not to respond.

"Hmm?" she answered, too love-tapped to move her lips.

"Katherine?"

She opened her eyes and lifted her face to look at him.

"What?"

"Nothing. I just wanted to see if you'd answer to the same name twice in a row," he said, grinning slow and lazy. He yelped and squirmed when she rubbed a knuckle up and down his ribs. Then he chuckled. "It's weird to fall in love with one name and be in love with another."

"You love Corrie's name?" she asked, looking hurt.

"Only because I thought it was your name," he said, and quickly added, "I *love* you. But in my head it sounds strange to me to be thinking, I love Katherine. All those times I thought of you, I'd think, I want to undress Corrie, real slow. And I want to touch her, everywhere. And I want to kiss Corrie and be so far inside of her that I'll never find my way back. I thought I'd be doing all those things to Corrie, not Katherine."

"So, when you think of me, you want to make love to her?"

"No. It's just the names. They're all mixed up in my head."

"So, you have Corrie and me mixed up. You don't know which of us you're making love to?" she asked, curbing a grin as she watched his facial expression change. He wasn't sure if he was filling a hole or digging one.

"No," he said carefully, watching the fading light of late afternoon glimmer warm in her eyes. "That's not what I meant. It wouldn't have mattered if you'd used Quinn's name, it would have still been you I was thinking about. You I was falling in love with."

"But not my name. Not Katherine. Why don't you like my name?"

"I do!" he said, frustrated, struggling to change his position to see her more clearly. "Katherine is a fine name. In fact, I think it suits your personality better than either Corrie or Quinn, but that doesn't have anything to do with what I was saying."

"Which was . . . ?"

"You, just you, were the woman playing around in my mind, but I kept thinking of you as Corrie. Now that I know who you are, it's hard to get used to thinking of you as Katherine."

"So, you were thinking of me as Corrie, and now that you know who we are, it's hard for you to think of me."

He moaned, dropping his forehead to her chest in near defeat. He felt her body shaking with laughter and came up fighting.

"You little . . . lawyer," he sputtered, pinning her body beneath his, clamping his hands about her wrists. "Look at you. So beautiful, with all that dark hair spread out on my pillow and those wonderful blue eyes of yours laughing at me. And then there's that lawyer's mouth, so sweet and so clever and so good at taking everything I say, turning it around, and spitting it back at me. I can't believe I fell for that." He took a moment to appreciate the view, then said, "I do believe I'm going to have to request an appeal here."

"What kind of an appeal?" she asked, growing excited and nervous at once.

"The kind where you throw yourself on my mercy and I don't have any."

"Mistrial," she called out playfully when he nuzzled his face to her neck. "Your intentions are predisposed toward me."

"You got that straight," he murmured, his lips brushing against her neck, his tongue driving her crazy as it swirled across her skin. He circled her throat with tiny kisses interspersed between his words. "The first time you looked at me and blushed like a schoolgirl, my intentions were . . . predisposed."

"You remember that? You noticed?"

His mouth moseyed down the valley between her breasts. "After that, I began to notice everything about you. The way you smell." He kissed the tip of her nose, then bent to her right breast. "The way you move." He suckled gently, then vigorously. Katherine arched her back and gasped with pleasure. "The sound of your voice."

With her hands shackled by his, she stretched her body, offering herself in unabridged enjoyment. Greedily, he took what she submitted, then demanded more.

She felt trapped inside her body. Her mind was gone, having whirled off into an abyss of thoughtless abandon sometime earlier. Muscles ached with longing, and nerve endings sizzled with delight. Like waves on a beach, her strength would swell and ebb away. She would struggle to put an end to the wondrous torment, then fall back in surrender to his every whim.

With her limbs spread wide, impatient and welcoming, he knelt between her knees, poising himself above her.

"Open your eyes," he said, his voice low and strained. When she could, she tried to focus on his face. He smiled and looked deep into dark blue pools of ecstasy. "Who do I love?"

"Me," she said. She could see it in his expression. That, and much more.

"Does anything else matter?"

"No."

Their words hung in the air as he took her. They mingled with their gasping breaths, their moans of long-awaited satisfaction, their cries of completion. Then they merged with their sighs of contentment.

In that moment, nothing did matter. Not their names. Not their faces. Not their pasts or even their future. It didn't matter that physical love between two humans was as common as snow in the Rockies.

In that moment, they were like snowflakes. Two among zillions—as different as they were alike. Two among zillions, who, through fate or design, chanced to touch, to connect and fuse as one. Two among zillions—changed forever, unique and unmatchable.

"Hey," Peter said sometime later when their skin had cooled and their racing pulses had slowed to bare life-support speed. She felt him move beside her, drawing the bed linens up over their bodies, tucking them close about her shoulders as he whispered in her ear. "Are you asleep?"

"Yes."

"Too bad," he said. "I wanted to tell you that I think you're terrific."

She rolled into his embrace, all but purring with contentment. She palmed his face, kissed him sweetly, and said, "I think you're pretty terrific too."

"So, we're a pair, then," he said, looking a little doubtful and in need of some assurance.

Katherine was touched. Peter's uncertainty was entirely unexpected. His vulnerability was heartrending. She knew that even the strongest male ego needed a little encouragement and pampering now and again— but Peter's libido? After what they'd just shared?

"We're definitely a pair," she said from the bottom of her heart.

"Great." He fell back into the pillows in extreme relief, then quickly came forward again, troubled and confused. "What did you say your name was again?"

She gasped.

He grinned.

"Gotcha."

SEVEN

In the weeks that followed, Katherine fell into a deceptive frame of mind entitled Life As It Should Be.

And why not? She won two of her three pro bono cases and earned the firm a very nice commission in a settlement with a pharmaceutical company.

When schedules allowed, she met Peter for lunch. Or if the gods were smiling, they'd take a room at the nearest hotel and get fast food on their way back to the office.

Days were long for both of them, but nighttime was theirs alone. Sometimes they'd meet at his suite, sometimes her apartment. Sometimes they'd head straight for the bed and sleep. Sometimes they'd head straight for the bed . . . and not sleep.

All the time, they'd talk.

"One of my all-time favorites is the '55 version of *East of Eden*. I cry every time I see it," he said.

The credits ran through on the television. Peter

used the remote to turn the set off, narrowly avoiding a third viewing of a used car commercial.

"And *Casablanca* doesn't tear you up?"

"It doesn't have a happy ending."

"Sure it does," she said. "Ilsa goes off with Victor where she belongs, and Rick and Louie go off to fight the Germans."

"Why does she belong with Victor? Because Victor and Rick think so? She wanted to stay with Rick. She was still in love with him."

They were turning off lights on their way to the bedroom. Katherine was amazed at what a soft touch he was. She liked it, but she was still amazed. *She* was far more practical.

"But she loved Victor, too, and he needed her more than Rick did. Besides, if she'd stayed with Rick, she'd have ended up in a concentration camp," she said.

"She didn't love Victor, she admired him—idealized him. And Victor's dedication to the resistance shouldn't have had anything to do with Ilsa. *And* Rick was a very sharp guy. He never would have gotten caught, and he wouldn't have let Ilsa get caught either."

"You just like *East of Eden* better because it's about twin boys," Katherine said, aggravated. "I suppose you think you're the good one."

He was aghast. "That guy was nuts, like John. I'm the smart one, the normal one." He wagged his brows at her. "The bad one who gets the girl in the end."

———❦———❦———

The door to Suite 819 flew open seconds after she knocked.

"Where the hell have you been?" he asked, his expression and tone of voice a precarious mixture of anxiety and anger. "It's been hours. I've been worried sick."

"I told you this morning that I'd be later than usual."

"You did?"

"Yes. You were looking for your shoes and I was ready to leave? I told you and you said you'd probably be late too? You were meeting with some contractors?"

"Right. They canceled."

"May I come in?" she asked, amused by his chagrin as he reached to pull her inside. "I'm glad you missed me."

"I've been missing you all day." He kissed her and kicked the door closed at the same time. "Where have you been?"

"To hell and back," she said, staggering as she tried to lift arms that were weighed down by shopping bags. "Lord & Taylor had a sale."

He was smiling when he took an armload of bags, then whistled his surprise at how heavy they were.

"This must be some guilt trip you're on," he said, amazed.

"Guilt trip? What makes you think I'm feeling guilty about something?"

"Didn't you tell me you went shopping whenever you felt bad about not being poor, or something along that line?"

She laughed. "If I were feeling guilty, it might be because I never need a good excuse to go shopping. However, I'm not feeling guilty, even though I did have a good excuse this time."

"This should be good," he said, chuckling, taking the second load of packages to stack them on top of the first beside a chair in the foyer. He turned to her, his eyes sparkling with merriment. He motioned to the small mountain. "There's an excuse for this?"

"I needed some new underthings."

"All this is new underwear?" he asked. His eyes grew round with wonder, and his mouth fell open in shock. He thought he'd died and gone to Men's World, where footballs, tool belts, and women's underwear were religious icons, symbolizing man's greatest achievements. He wanted to genuflect and worship openly, but suddenly remembered . . . he was sworn to secrecy.

"Don't be ridiculous," she was saying. "I found this gorgeous coral suit, and then I needed shoes to go with it, and while I was looking for those, I found a pair that'll go perfectly with the outfit Quinn gave me when it turned out to be too small for her and not short enough for Corrie. Have you eaten? There's a darling sweater in there, too, somewhere," she said, turning away. "Do you mind if I order something up to eat? I'm starving."

Peter watched her walk into the living room and out of sight, then glanced back at her booty, completely disgruntled.

What? No show-and-tell? No fashion show?

"Hey, wait a second," he called, chasing after her. "You didn't try all this stuff on at the store, did you?"

"Christmas is my favorite holiday."

It was a lazy Sunday morning. Decked out in sweats and socks, she had his feet and a truckload of briefs she needed to read in her lap.

"It's just another day for me," he said from behind his newspaper. "I like St. Patrick's Day."

"Wesley isn't an Irish name."

"Peter is."

"It is not."

"It doesn't matter anyway. On St. Patrick's Day you can be as Irish as you want, and I like to go all out."

"You need children. Quinn's kids make the whole Christmas season seem like magic, like when we were little. Little ones make all the difference."

"I will if you will," he said, lowering his paper to look at her.

"You will what?"

"Have children." He looked inspired. "Hey, we could have kids together. I'll help you make them, you carry and deliver them, I'll take them to school every morning, and together we'll support them for the rest of our lives. What do you say?"

"How can you say that?" Peter asked, standing to help clear away their dinner dishes. "That's communism, and Russia's a perfect example that it doesn't work."

"I'm not saying that the government should support the homeless indefinitely," she said, following him into the kitchen—the smallest room in her apartment. "But until we can convince big business to keep production inside the United States, and Americans to buy American, and broaden our labor base again, the government has to do something—certainly more than they're doing now. Those people need help."

"What manufacturer in his right mind is going to pay minimum wage in the U.S. when he can get his product out for a tenth of the cost in a third world nation?" he asked, playing devil's advocate just to see her eyes light up.

"One who cares about his country," she said, angry that the world couldn't be the ideal place she wanted it to be. "Do you want to rinse dishes or wipe counters?"

"Wipe counters." She threw a wet dishrag at him. "How come you're mad at me? I hire American."

"You're the only one here," she said, then sent him an apologetic smile. "I get so tired of living in that gray space between how things should be and the way they are."

"You want me to get that?"

"What?"

"The phone's ringing."

Not one to miss a phone call, she went silent to listen.

"No. I'll get it."

He finished clearing the table and wiped it off, then started rinsing dishes.

Everything about Katherine Asher was passionate. The way she thought. The way she worked. The way she played. The way she made love. A strong woman with strong convictions, and he wouldn't want her any other way. She made him think about things that he hadn't paid much attention to before. He found himself having opinions and concerns he hadn't realized he had. She could arouse his thoughts and emotions, as well as his body, on any subject that happened to come their way. She made life seem important, exciting, worth getting passionate about. And for someone as easygoing and take-it-as-it-comes as Peter Wesley, that was no small feat.

"Damn, damn," she said, coming back into the kitchen, furious and frustrated. "And double damn."

"Bad news?"

She was impatient when she looked at him.

"Just a guess."

"Belle's in jail."

"Belle? Belle Gumph?"

"Malicious mischief, destruction of public property, assault on a city official, and resisting arrest."

"Belle Gumph?"

"She poured dish detergent into the fuel lines of two bulldozers, set fire to several traffic barricades, hit a city building inspector with a wooden spoon, and bit her arresting officer."

"Belle Gumph?"

"We filed an appeal against Judge Everly's eminent domain decision. It seems that sometime since I last spoke with her, Belle took it upon herself to move into one of those old buildings. I suspect she wanted to make sure nothing happened to the buildings before we could state our case in court."

He shook his head sympathetically. He, of course, knew about the appeal and had purposefully not discussed it with her. He hadn't wanted to put the nasty taste of business into the pleasure between them. Now it seemed he had no choice.

"There is no case to state. There never is in a situation like this. The individual's claim is sacrificed for the greater good. She's wasting her time and money, and you're letting her," he said unemotionally and with brutal honesty.

He might as well have waved a red flag at her.

"*Any time* there is a conflict of interest, there is a case to be stated. Belle has every right in the world to keep those buildings. She's the one who's paid the taxes and maintained those buildings for the last forty years. Not the city."

"That whole neighborhood is ready to fall into the river."

She went silent for a moment.

"Do we want to fight about this?" she asked, making it clear that the choice was his.

He looked at her thoughtfully. "No. Do what you have to do."

"And you'll do the same?"

Gravely he nodded. Their gazes met and exchanged silent concerns that what they did for a living could very possibly interfere in their private lives.

"I have to go get Belle out of jail," she said, turning to leave him.

"Katherine." She looked at him. "We'll take it as it comes. We'll work it out. Okay?"

"Okay."

She left, and he was still in the kitchen holding a dripping dish in one hand.

Yessireebob, everything about Katherine Asher was passionate. That quality that he so loved in her, that he respected and admired about her, was the same quality that was now clamping down on his heart like cast iron tongs with pointed tips, he discovered.

The argument that hadn't quite happened was only a preview of what was to come. He knew it wasn't over. He could feel it in his bones. Katherine always finished what she started, whether it was the last few lines of the newspaper article she was reading before work in the morning or the final touches to the brief she was preparing for court or the Sunday crossword puzzle. She finished everything.

One way or another, and with all the best intentions between them, they'd finish that argument. He could see it coming in his mind's eye as he turned to the sink to finish up the dishes. Like two trains coming head on. It would be unintentional, of course—who in their right mind would put two trains going in opposite directions on the same track?

He sighed loudly as he turned off the water and started for the bathroom, hoping to find some antacid.

EIGHT

"What the hell is this?"

John strode into Katherine's office the next morning waving a piece of paper and all but foaming at the mouth after he'd been made to wait for twenty minutes to see her. At least she was pretty sure it was John.

"Let me see?" she asked calmly, standing and extending her hand for the paper. "Why, it looks to me like a restraining order, Mr. Wesley."

A subtle movement at her office door caught her eye. Peter stood quietly, holding up the door frame with his shoulder. He winked her a good-morning-again-and-you-sure-do-look-good wink, and then let his expression go blank and unreadable.

"You can't do this," John said, his voice straining with control. "That property has been claimed by the city, legal and fair, and we have a contract to get this project underway and done as soon as possible."

"You should have thought of that before you started harassing my client and her tenants, John."

"Harassing? I'm too busy tearing down warehouses to harass anybody."

"Right. That's why you're paying three men to run the motors on the heavy equipment all night so no one on the block can sleep. And why you put up road barricades to keep taxis out and the Meals on Wheels people from making their rounds. The people in those buildings were virtually being held prisoner in their own homes. Not to mention that there was a city inspector of one thing or another visiting those buildings twice, sometimes three times a day. Please, don't play innocent. You and I both know how these things work and why we got a restraining order against you."

"Your client is senile." He was trying so hard to stay calm and rational.

"And you're a bully, but let's not get into name-calling here, shall we?" She stepped back behind her desk as if to go on with her business and forget him. "You're free to do what you must down there, John. Just steer clear of Belle Gumph's buildings, and cease and desist any and all acts of harassment until we can settle this in court. By the way, as long as you're here, would you like to schedule a day for your deposition?"

John glared at her, then turned to Peter with a will-you-do-something-with-her frown. Peter shrugged and grimaced helplessly. He watched his brother stomp past him and out of the office, then turned his head to smile broadly and intimately at Katherine.

"I forgot to ask if you wanted Subgum or Moo Shu tonight."

"Aren't you mad at me too?" she asked.

"Nah. I'm crazy about ya."

"I'm serious."

"So am I."

"I can't blame him for being angry, and I can't help thinking that I'm interfering with your business too," she reminded him.

"You're doing your job. This isn't the first or the last restraining order we've had."

"This could get a lot worse before it's over."

"Then John and I'll have to take turns blowing up. I don't want him to have a stroke."

"Peter," she said, stepping to his side. "Be serious. I'm worried."

He pushed himself to an upright position and reached for her.

"We'll be all right," he said, rubbing her forearms to comfort her. "We'll deal with it as it comes, remember?"

She nodded, but she was still worried.

Love was as fragile as it was powerful. If it could be shattered by things as simple as toothpaste tubes and hair in the sink, what could a lawsuit do to it?

Depositions were a part of Katherine's life. Not a favorite part, but certainly one she understood and tolerated because of the court time they saved; and it was always good to know ahead of time which questions to ask in front of the judge—and which to avoid. . . .

"That whole neighborhood is rat infested. All you can do is level it and start over," said the exterminator who would be called as a part of Belle's defense.

"Please don't offer any opinions, Mr. Robanichek. My question was, to your knowledge, are the buildings belonging to Belle Gumph infested with bugs or rodents?"

"No way."

"How do you know this?"

"Mrs. Gumph keeps us on retainer."

"What does that mean?"

"You know what that means. I explained it to you last week when we first talked."

"I need it for the record, Mr. Robanichek."

He let loose a long-suffering sigh. "It means that we inspect and treat both her buildings three times a year, come hell or high water."

"Come hell or high water?"

"She keeps track of us. Four months, and if we're even a day late, she comes all the way down to the office downtown and jumps all over us."

Expert witnesses, testifying to the state and condition of the buildings, didn't need an attorney to give a deposition. They were merely offering their professional opinions and couldn't be prosecuted for them later. However, witnesses directly involved with the case were encouraged to hire protection ag..nst later prosecution. And they were allowed, encouraged even, by the opposing team to say anything and everything that came to mind regarding the case.

"Is it common practice to inspect a building for code violations two and three times a week, Mr. Moore?"

"It happens."

"As a common practice?"

"No."

"Under what conditions would a building be inspected more than once a month, or even more than once a week?"

"We inspect the buildings once a year or at specific request. If there are violations, we return in thirty to ninety days to follow up," he recited nervously from rote.

"To your knowledge, were the buildings at 114 and 357 River Street ever cited for violations?"

"Yes, ma'am. In 1987, 357 needed a new heating system."

"Was the furnace replaced?"

"Yes, ma'am."

"Have there been any violations since then?"

"No, ma'am."

"In the past several weeks, have inspectors been sent to either or both of those addresses more than once a week?"

"Yes, ma'am."

"Since there were no violations, am I to assume these visits were made by request?"

After a quick look at his attorney, he answered, "You could assume that, yes, ma'am."

"By whom were these requests made?"

"Some people at the River Vista Project."

"Can you be more specific?"

"Well," he said, scanning the ceiling as he thought it over. "One of the Wesley brothers suggested the frequent inspections as a . . . a form of annoyance. The other brother said, 'at least once a week,' but I don't know which said what. It's hard to tell those two apart. Anyway, I figured the old lady would get the message faster if we came even more often than that."

"So, there was a conspiracy between the River Vista people and the city to heckle and hound Mrs. Gumph away from her buildings?"

She was as angry with Peter for his part in the devious plan as she was with John—as she would have been with anyone stooping to such dishonorable means to cheat an old woman out of her property.

"Are you going to stay mad at me forever?" Peter asked that evening, reaching out to massage the cold shoulder he'd been getting since he'd arrived at her apartment.

"I'm thinking about it." She didn't look up from the *ABA Journal* she was trying to read.

"Come on, Katherine. It's business. It shouldn't have anything to do with us." He was beginning to hear two distinct train whistles blowing in the distance. His heart cringed.

"How can I feel the way I feel about you, knowing that you're a low-down—"

"Ah-ah," he said in a warning tone. "You feel the way you do about me because you know I'm *not* a low-down anything. I'm trying to do the job I was hired to do. Just like you. Belle's fighting a court decision, and we're fighting back. It's that simple." He bent low to search the pouty expression on her face. "You surely didn't expect us to roll over and play dead while you and Belle Gumph diddle around in court? We have men on the payroll who'd be getting paid to stand around and pick their nose all day while we wait for a decision that as far as we're concerned has already been made once. We'd have expensive equipment standing idle. We'd be laying foundations in the middle of winter, when everything takes longer to do and set up. Believe me, the cost and inconvenience to Belle and the rest of her tenants is nothing compared to what it would have cost us to do nothing."

"You held up the Meals on Wheels people," she said accusingly.

"No, we didn't. And I don't care what Belle Gumph says about that," he said emphatically, still refusing to apologize for his actions. "We're not stupid. We knew there were elderly people in those buildings. We wouldn't have risked the bad press for the project by letting anything happen to any of them because of the barricades. Only half the street was closed, and there were taxis and emergency vehicles up and down that street all day long," he said. "She's mad because we had the buses rerouted and she had to walk two blocks to catch one."

She glanced at him from the corner of her eye.

"You're sure about that?" she asked, wanting to give him the benefit of the doubt. What he'd done wasn't illegal. In fact, it was a common practice in similar situations. She wanted—needed—to think his actions weren't so very terrible. "What about running the bulldozers all night?"

"I'm sure that was very annoying," he said, sitting back on the couch, righteously declining to beg and plead for forgiveness for something he considered to be fair play.

She let his lack of repentance trivialize the incident further, because she trusted the basic goodness in his character.

She was quiet for a long time, thinking, weighing . . . compromising. Finally she let loose an enormous sigh. "I should tell Belle to get a different attorney to handle this. I'm biased."

"No kidding," he grumbled. "Right now, nothing would make me happier than to have you out of this mess completely. Aside from the friction it's causing between us, I think your bias is the best chance that old lady has of keeping those buildings."

"Why do you say that?"

"Because I know you. You'll work twice as hard as you usually do—four times harder than any other attorney—to get Belle a fair hearing. *And* to prove that your professional judgment hasn't been colored by me."

She could see that happening already.

"And what if we win? How will you feel?"

He shrugged, but he didn't look at her. "I'm a big boy. I can take my lumps."

That was probably true, she thought. He was a take-your-lumps-and-paint-them-red sort of person, someone who would make the best of any situation. He wasn't like John, who would be furious. And he wasn't like her, who took losing personally, like a not-so-private failure.

"What about you?" he asked, watching her. "What if you lose again? Will you microwave my new tooth-brush in effigy?"

"I might," she warned him, her eyes serious and worried. "I'm not a very good sport about these things."

"No kidding," he said again, his lips curling into a teasing smile. "When I used to hear that opposites attract, I never dreamed it meant that I'd end up with someone like you."

"Someone like me?" She frowned suspiciously. "What does that mean, someone like me?"

"It means that I'm surprised that I'd fall for some-one who takes everything so seriously, who cares about everything, worries about everything."

"What's wrong with caring?"

"Absolutely nothing. I like it. I love that part of

you. Watching you get worked up about something excites me. I . . . it's hard to explain, but you make me want to care too." He snatched the magazine from her fingers and tossed it to the floor, using her hands to draw her toward him.

"I'm not a crusader, Katherine. I don't feel as if I can change the world, so I don't try. I always thought it was enough to make my contribution to the earth aesthetically, through my buildings, and to keep the tiny part of life that belongs to me on the cleanest, smoothest, and easiest path I could find." He skimmed the back of his hand across her cheek, marveling at its delicate softness. "Watching you leap the potholes and cleaning up the litter and sweating on the uphill tracks and trying to keep your balance in the curves, amazes me. It fascinates me. I wonder why you do it. I wonder why you bother, when your path could be as simple as mine. I think and wonder all the time. I try to look at the world from your perspective, and I see things. Things I've heard about, things I knew existed, but I never really *saw* before."

He leaned against the back of the couch and went silent for a moment.

"I don't think I ever wanted to see before," he admitted thoughtfully. "I've stood and looked at both of those old buildings of Belle's and wondered, what is it about Belle and these two old heaps of brick and mortar that stir Katherine's emotions? Why does she care about them almost as much as she cares about me?"

"And have you come to any conclusions?" she asked softly, watching him the way she might a confused teenager who was suddenly feeling and noticing the changes in his body, and in the world in general.

"You mean, other than that you might be a little crazy?" he asked, and grinned, stalling as he prepared his answer.

"Yes. Other than that," she said, returning his smile with great understanding.

"No. No conclusions, not yet. But maybe some understanding. Certainly some awareness." He paused. "And a choice."

"To do what?"

"To look at the cards as I see them or to flip them over and see both sides."

"And what about acting on what you see?" she asked gently. As if it were a physical thing, she could feel her heart reaching out to his.

He shrugged and shook his head before he looked at her.

"I guess that remains to be seen, huh?" he said. He was feeling a little overexposed, a little self-impelled to take actions he wasn't prepared to take to impress her —and a lot hungry. "Let's order take-out. I'm starving."

"Sure, if you want, but I cooked," she said temptingly.

"You did?" he asked, doubly impressed. She rarely had time to cook with her work schedule, and she'd been angry with him earlier. The generosity of her spirit astounded him.

"I was so mad, I was going to sit and eat it in front of you. But now I guess I might be persuaded to share it with you."

He tried to look disheartened. "Well, what do I have to do to persuade you?"

"Oh, I'm sure you can think of something," she said, scooting closer to him. She outlined her lips with the tip of her tongue suggestively.

"Let's see. I could run faster than a speeding bullet for you."

"Too tiring."

"Swim an ocean for you?"

"Too long."

"Lasso a star for you?"

"Too ecologically unsound."

"Sit on a flagpole for you?"

"Ow! Too painful."

"Wrestle an alligator for you?"

"Too stupid."

"Jump a tall building for you?"

"I'd rather you jumped me."

"No problem."

NINE

"This is heaven," Katherine said on a sigh, her face raised to the early morning sun, a gentle breeze rustling her dark hair.

Sunday morning they had driven to the marina at the mouth of the Safran River, where Peter had his boat moored. After a leisurely brunch, they had sailed out of the bay, through the quiet weekend traffic, to the ocean. They dropped anchor when they could no longer see land and reveled in the idea that they were completely alone, isolated from the rest of the world and not likely to be disturbed.

"No phones. No people. Just you and me and the water and the sky."

"And those damned birds circling like vultures," Peter said, growling at the sea gulls from his prone position beside her.

His baby, a twenty-six-foot cabin cruiser, was out of dry dock, and he was once again King of the Sea.

He lay face down on a mat at Katherine's feet, soaking in the sun's warmth through his shirt, letting the wind tickle the small hairs on his neck, listening to the soft pleasured sounds Katherine was making as she wallowed in relaxation . . . and, of course, those damned birds.

"You feed 'em out of the kindness of your heart, then they turn around and poop all over your boat so their pals know where to go for a handout," he said, his face in the bend of his arm. "They're worse than any dog I ever met."

"Not much on animals, are you?" she said, slouching in the deck chair, eyes closed.

"Not when they poop on my boat."

She chuckled. "You know, I don't think I've ever spent the night on a boat before. It was wonderful. I thought the boat would rock more than it did, but I hardly noticed it. And what I did feel was very comforting."

"Like a mother rocking her baby."

"Yes, in a way. Maybe," she said, mulling it. She heard him move on the mat.

He rolled to one side, supporting his head with his hand to look up at her.

"We'll do this again. We'll take some time for ourselves and spend a whole week on board."

"Two weeks," she said, lolling her head to one side to smile at him.

"A month."

She sighed.

"Just the two of us. We'll lie around all day long," he said. "I'll fish and you can read. We'll only stop when we want to, and then we'll find some romantic restaurant and dance until our feet ache. We'll walk back to the docks under the stars, barefoot, along the beach. We'll make love until dawn, and then we'll let the water slowly rock us to sleep." She purred contentedly. He was ready to weigh anchor and start their vacation at that very moment, but . . .

He came to a sitting position and stroked her arm, reaching high into the sleeve of her T-shirt to feel her soft, sun-warmed skin.

"I say we stop pretending to be a couple of responsible, mature adults. I say we chuck it all and leave now. What do you say?"

"I second that motion," she said lazily.

"You can't." He showed her a mask of considerable disappointment. "I was counting on you to be the practical one who reminds me that if I don't go to work once in a while, I'll be dead in the water—one way or another."

"No, I checked," she said. "Most of the backers for your project are legitimate business types. The worse they'd do is sue your pants off, and you won't need them where we're going."

"There's still John to consider. He wouldn't think twice about ordering me a pair of cement shoes."

"We'll take him with us. He needs a vacation more than we do." She absently halted the hand slipping up inside her shorts. "And if he bothers us too much, we'll use him as shark bait."

He chuckled in agreement. "Okay. But what'll we do for money then? This isn't a sailboat, you know."

"You mean this thing doesn't run on love?" It was her turn to look disillusioned. "Who'd buy a boat like this that doesn't run on love vapors?"

"Someone who hadn't met the woman he wanted to run away with yet, I guess."

She smiled at him. If her heart were a piece of wood, Peter would be a boreworm, she thought, drilling a thousand little entrances, tunneling for easy access, making his home at the core. She could almost feel him digging his way in, becoming a part of her. It felt as inevitable and instinctive as any act of nature.

"Oh, all right," she said, giving in. "I'll be the bad guy and insist we go back now."

"Thank you, thank you, thank you," he said, overly sincere. He came to his knees to wax poetically, "I am a weak and lowly man with no character, wholly undeserving of a stout-willed, clear-thinking, sturdy woman such as yourself."

"Sturdy woman?"

"Strong and solid."

"Let's leave sturdy out and go with stout-willed and clear-thinking. Sturdy makes me sound like a tree."

He bent over her and pressed his lips to hers.

"Whatever you say, oh, wonderful woman of mine. For even though your roots run deep into my heart and the heavens smile down upon you, we know you are no tree."

She groaned and gave a pretty good imitation of retching on his sweetness. He laughed and ruffled her hair before he climbed to the pilot's seat. She watched him, smiling. He had a great tush.

"Oh, captain," she called, lifting a finger in the air.

He loved being called captain, and as such, always responded in character.

He turned to face her with an authoritative glower, and lifting his fists to his hips, waited for her question.

"Do you have the time, sir?"

He glanced at his watch. "Two bells and all is well," he called. She'd received a boring lesson on ship's bells and presently used her fingers to calculate that it was about nine o'clock, while he continued to speak. "We'll be home and I'll be swabbin' ya down in the shower in two hours. Where do you want to go for lunch, me matey?"

"No lunch today," she said, watching him turn to fiddle with levers and push buttons. She could tell that he felt easy at the helm of his prized possession. His movements were casual, decisive, and masterful— much as they were with everything he did, she pondered, including their lovemaking. "I'm meeting with Belle at one to prepare her for her deposition this afternoon. I don't want her flying off the handle and taking a bite out of your attorney."

"Are you sure I can't come watch?" he asked, raising his voice to be heard over the anchor tows.

"She's a pain in the butt, but I like ol' Belle. I like her spunk."

"Is that what you call it? Spunk?"

"Ah-ah. Careful," he said, turning his head to grin at her. "I see a lot of her in you. You'll probably grow up and be an old pain in the butt too."

She didn't *not* like the idea of being an old woman who stood up for her rights and fought back at injustice. She didn't *not* like the idea of being a feisty old lady who could terrify anyone she wanted to. She didn't even *not* like the idea of growing old, so long as she didn't have to do it alone—so long as Peter would grow old with her.

Except for the night they discussed children, she hadn't given much thought to having Peter in her life for a time span that equaled forever. It had been enough to simply love him in the here and now— the here and now filling her so completely with happiness.

She closed her eyes and tried to picture Peter with no teeth and less hair. The powerful engines beneath the boat turned over and hummed loudly. She visualized her own hair graying and thinning, her body stooping and sagging, and wondered if Peter would still love her. The wind picked up and blew harder as the boat began to move. She wanted to die in her sleep one night, next to Peter. She wanted to go first, because she knew she couldn't bear losing him. Not now. Not in a hundred years. Not ever.

It was a few minutes before she felt the boat gently

turning away from the sun. And a few more minutes still before she heard the engines begin to sputter and cough. She opened her eyes to see Peter pushing levers and buttons and tapping glass-covered gauges.

"Is something wrong?" she called, her voice too loud now that the engines went suddenly silent. "What's happening?"

"I don't know," he said, trying to restart the engines, getting a worthless clicking sound for his efforts. "I'm losing fuel pressure."

Using the rails for balance, he jumped to the deck, moving from side to side to check the port and starboard engines. He scrambled over the upholstered seat to lie on his belly and examine the stern.

"Don't panic," he said. "I might be able to fix it."

"Fix what?"

"We're leaking gas." He opened a panel in the floor and began turning valves to cut off the flow of gasoline. "It might be a tear in the line or . . . or something else I can fix."

Katherine was sitting up now, on the edge of her chair. She looked for land or another seafaring vessel and saw nothing but water on all sides.

Peter, having decided to remain calm and collected in the face of this hopefully minor disaster, lowered himself from the pilot's deck once more with a small metal box in hand.

"We'll be fixed up and on our way in no time," he said, giving her a gentle rub on the back as he walked past her.

"A man with a toolbox. Always a comforting sight," she said, also determined to stay cheerful, even as nervous juices churned in her stomach.

Time passed.

"Do you have another roll of tape?" she asked, watching him work. He had the stern casing elevated, his back bowed over the seat, his head in the works. "There's not much left on that roll, and you still need to mend the end you cut off."

Her backseat mechanics didn't bother him. He was used to having John at his back, worrying aloud over his shoulder.

What did irritate him was the impatience and lack of faith in her voice. He was a very clever fellow. But he wasn't a mechanic. He was doing his best, as fast as he could.

"It'll do," he said simply.

"There's gas all over in there. It won't explode when you try to start the engine again, will it?"

"It might." But he didn't think so.

"What if the tape doesn't hold?"

"It will."

"All the way back to the marina?"

"At least until we get back into the traffic. Then we can send off a flare if we have to."

"Let's send one off now."

"We're not sure anyone will see it."

"We're not sure someone won't."

"True," he said slowly, a niggling ache forming in his temples as he fought his anger. "But if we shoot off the flares when we're not sure someone might see them and no one does, what will we do for flares when someone passes by?"

"We don't need to shoot them all off. Just one or two."

"I have three."

"Okay, one. We'll save the other two."

"Fine. Go shoot off a flare."

She could tell by his voice that something was wrong.

"This isn't like the asking-for-directions thing, is it? Men signal for help when they really need it, don't they?" When he didn't answer, she continued, "We used to think it was funny when my dad would drive around for hours looking for an address rather than stop at a gas station and ask for directions, but we never ran out of gas or broke down or anything."

He tore at the tape with a vengeance, then straightened his back and turned to look at her. If he hadn't been briny deep in love with her and if he hadn't seen the anxiety in her eyes, he might have thrown her overboard.

"I don't have any trouble asking for help or directions when I need them," he said, his jaw tight with control. "See if you can find a pair of needle-nosed pliers in there, will you?"

She bent over the toolbox obediently. She was still worried about the tension in his voice. "My dad used to cuss and shout when he had trouble fixing something. You can, too, if you want. I'll certainly understand."

"Thank you, but I don't think it's necessary just yet."

"Oh." She sounded surprised when she handed him the pliers. "I thought you might be having trouble. It's taking you a long time."

"Do you want to do this?" he asked, his restraint slipping a bit.

"What do I know about boat engines?"

"They're all pretty much alike. If you can fix any motor, you can fix this one."

"Well, I can't."

"Can't what?"

"Fix any motor."

"Then please be quiet while I try."

That stung a little, but at least she knew that she wasn't imagining his stress. He finally did give in to cursing when an attempt to start up the engines failed. Not the blue streaks she remembered her father producing, but little puffs of dark angry smoke that seemed to hang heavy over the back of the boat.

More time passed.

The sun rose high in the sky, beating down on Peter's now bare back. He was hot and sweaty. He taped and screwed and unscrewed and adjusted this piece and that part to no avail. It was tiring and frustrating work—especially with Katherine pacing the width of the boat and sighing every three minutes.

She was hot and sweaty . . . and bored and worried.

She looked at Peter's watch, now hanging loosely

on her wrist. He had long since given up on ship's bells and given the watch to her to save time. Apparently, she'd asked about it too often.

Anyway, it was almost noon, and thoughts of Belle Gumph were looming bigger and thicker in her mind by the second.

"Would you like a cold drink?" she asked, breaking the silence so abruptly that it startled him.

"Thanks," he said. He continued to toil while she took a soft drink from the cooler, popped it, then sat on the seat beside him.

"Are you hungry?"

He took a sip before answering.

"No," he said, looking at her for a long moment. "Why haven't you asked about the radio yet?"

Taken aback, she had to think about her answer. She had thought about the radio, she'd even glanced at it a couple of times. She shrugged finally. "I don't know. I guess I assumed that if you thought it would help, you'd have used it."

He smiled and half chuckled. Turning, he sat on the seat next to her. "Thank you for that." He sighed and the stiffness in his shoulders and expression drained away to defeat and regret. "Truth is, it's broken."

"Oh." She'd thought they were out of range or something equally stupid and technical. It hadn't occurred to her that anything on Peter's bright, shiny baby didn't work properly.

"I asked them to fix it before they put her back in the water, but they had to wait for a part and I . . . I was anxious to go out with you, and everything else checked out okay, and we weren't going far or for long . . . and, well, it's my fault. If I'd waited another week to get the radio fixed, we could have called for help hours ago. I'm sorry, Katherine."

Half of her understood completely, could even feel the urgency he'd felt to get away and be alone together. That part of her empathized with him, even admitted that she might have done the exact same thing in his place and absolved him of any serious wrongdoing.

However, the other half of her had spent the morning with thoughts of Belle Gumph, and that part of her was mad.

"I told you Saturday when we decided to do this how important Belle's deposition is," she said carefully, but unable to hide the fact that she was put out with the situation. "It's important for me to be there."

"I know. But maybe it won't be so bad after all," he said, looking for a bright side. "Belle would say whatever she wanted to say whether you were there or not. She'll do fine by herself."

She shook her head. "I wish I could see it that way."

"Why? What do you think'll happen?"

"She might refuse to take part in it without my being there, which is what I hope she does. But she'll also be in contempt of court, which won't look good and could get sticky. On the other hand, if she decides to go into the deposition without legal protection, your attorney could chew her up, or more likely, make her angry, and she'll either say too much or walk out. Either way, we'll be in trouble."

"Won't someone in your office notice you aren't there and do something? Get it postponed or something?"

"I hope so," she said, despondent. She drew her knees up under her chin, hugged her legs, and began to think aloud. "I'm not the only lawyer in the office with a full load though, and Mondays are hairy. The only ones who might notice I'm not there are Jean, and Lois, my clerk . . . but I asked her to do some research for me today, so she might not be there till late this afternoon." A sick expression crossed her face. "Ted Evens."

"Who's— Oh, your boss?"

She nodded absently, visualizing the carnage of her career. "Senior partner. Office Scrooge. When Jean notices I haven't shown up for Belle's deposition, she'll ask to reschedule, but if that doesn't work, she won't have any choice but to ask Ted to step in for me. He'll be furious. He'll ask questions. And if I answer honestly . . ." She groaned and let her head fall to her knees. "This couldn't look worse if you'd . . ."

. . . . planned it?

It was just a thought. Not even a thought, really. Just something that almost fell from her mouth.

"If I'd what?" he asked, suddenly wary.

She raised her head slowly and looked him straight

in the eyes. They were dark and fathomless, revealing no answers, no guilt, no innocence—only the challenge to finish her sentence.

"If I'd what, Katherine?" he asked again, swallowing hard as he grew rigid with pride and readied himself for a painful blow.

She was shaking her head in denial when something beyond his right ear caught her attention.

"Look! What's that?" she said, jumping to her feet, shielding her eyes from the sun with her hand to get a better look.

Peter took one look and was on his knees on the pilot's deck, rummaging through a drawer, then brandishing a flare gun.

"Do you think it's a boat? It looks like a cloud."

"It's a ship," he said, returning to her side, breathless. "They won't come this way, but if they see the flare they might radio for help."

It was like a red-tailed comet, soaring high into the sky, hovering for a moment, then splintering apart and falling into the sea.

"Will they signal back if they saw it?"

"How the hell should I know?"

They stood tense and waiting for what seemed like forever.

"Should we shoot off another? In case they didn't see the first one?"

The sound of the second flare was deafening and reverberated across the water over and over, softer and softer, until there was nothing but the gentle noise of the water lapping. Again they stood, hearts racing, waiting.

"I don't think I can see it anymore. Can you?"

"No," he said, his voice subdued. He draped his long body along several cushions, closed his eyes, and turned his face to the sun.

"If they saw the flares, how long do you think it will take for help to get here?"

"I have no idea."

"Maybe that's just as well," she said, stretching out across from him. "I won't know when to give up hope."

"Does it work that way with people too?"

"What?"

"After a certain amount of time or a specific amount of trouble or an exact quota of problems and misunderstandings, you just give up on them? Is that how it works?"

"How what works?"

She sat up to look at him. He sat up to face her.

"Do you really think that I stranded us here on purpose so you'd miss Belle Gumph's deposition?" he asked straight out.

No, that wasn't what she thought. For a moment she might have thought it possible of John—but even that idea had been hard to sustain.

However, in the split second it took for the notion to clear her mind, she'd hesitated, and the damage was done.

"You do, don't you?"

"No. I don't. I know you wouldn't—"

"You think I broke the radio and cut the fuel lines and screwed up whatever else is wrong with the motor, just so you'd miss that damn deposition," he said, his expression hurt and disbelieving.

"No. Truly, I didn't. I thought John might have done something, but—"

"John. John?" Now he was really getting steamed. He gave his locomotive full throttle, heading straight for hers. He was tired of waiting for the inevitable. They were going to have it out here and now and get it over with, settle the issue, once and for all. "You thought my brother sabotaged my boat? Why? To make you miss that stupid deposition?"

"Well, yes, but only for a second. I know he wouldn't do something—"

"Honey, you don't know anything," he said, standing to glower down at her. "First off, we don't work like that. We don't have to. We have city government on our side before we even agree to do a job, and nothing, *nothing* but an act of Congress can stop us. That includes you and Belle Gumph. You can take us to court all you want. You can spin your wheels in the justice system till your hair turns gray, and get depositions from every garbage inspector and bug catcher in town, and it isn't going to make a damn bit of difference to us."

"And your second point?" she asked quietly. He frowned. "You said, 'first off,' so what's your second point?"

Did he need a second point? He could have told her that he and his brother didn't stoop to tricks and subterfuge because they believed in fair play and were as honest and up-front as anyone in business for themselves could be. Or that they had pride and believed in hard work and in treating others as they liked to be treated. Or that for all their humanness, they weren't even half bad and that they believed in her right to fight the system as much as they believed in their own right to use it.

He could have told her that he loved her, that he trusted her to do what she thought was the right thing. He could have said that if she loved him, she could have trusted him not to interfere; she could have believed that he'd never purposefully hurt her—physically, emotionally, or professionally—and that he'd kill his own brother for trying.

He could have said any of those things, but it would have hurt too much.

"I don't need a second point. My first one will keep Belle Gumph dishing out legal fees till the turn of the century, if she lives that long."

"Oh! You are so smug," she said, taking instant umbrage with his supreme arrogance. "That's a typical big-business attitude. You and your pals in the government just take what you want and stomp all over people while you're doing it, and never think twice about it until someone tries to do it to you. Then you start screaming and yelling about your rights to this and your rights to that—the exact same rights you didn't pay any attention to when you were getting what you have in the first place—"

She yelped when he suddenly lunged at her, picked her up, and lifted her to stand on the padded bench behind her.

"That'll have to do," he said. "I'm fresh out of soapboxes, babe."

"Don't call me babe."

"Well, excuse me, Madam Counselor. But while you're up there, why don't you take a good look around. Big business feeds this country."

"Right." Her arms went akimbo. "That's why there are children starving in the streets, whole families living in cardboard boxes, and . . . Oh! . . . Oh!"

The boat pitched on a wave, throwing her off balance. She flapped her arms in a circular motion, trying to stay upright. He reached for her, grabbing her hips, but she was top-heavy by then and fell, screaming and terrified, into the bay.

The darkness was quite remarkable. The frigid temperature of the water hardly registered in her mind as she envisioned young Corrie and Quinn sitting on the edge of the pool in polka-dot suits, one blue, the other purple. She was looking up at them, through water, and they were laughing.

Had she ever mentioned to Peter that she'd taken swimming lessons? she wondered abstractedly. Had she remembered to tell him that she'd failed miserably at them? Did he know that she wouldn't float back to the surface? That she'd sink to the bottom of the bay like a rock, holding her breath until her lungs felt like bursting, waiting for him to come get her?

He was angry with her, but she knew he wouldn't let her die. However, it was taking him a long time to figure out that she wasn't going to surface, she decided, her thoughts coming to her like dreams, a collage of reality, fantasy, and memory.

Suddenly there was air and light and Peter's face leaning over the side of the boat. His arms were reaching out to her. It was her chance to tell him that she couldn't swim. She opened her mouth, gulped air into her lungs and water into her mouth, then slipped back into the darkness. Peter's face blurred and became distorted, and she was sorry she'd argued with him.

Sadness overwhelmed her, and she felt a rage burning in her soul. She wasn't ready to die. She could feel her arms and legs moving. She wanted to make love with Peter. She wanted to win Belle's buildings back from the city. She wanted to say . . . Lord, she still had so much to say! Her body flailed wildly against the tons of water surrounding her. She wasn't finished. She never left things undone. No one would believe she was dead. And what about her babies? She wanted babies. Peter's babies. She struck out at her massive enemy, fighting it, beating at it.

Peter's politics were all screwed up, but she loved him. She needed to tell him.

A gut-grabbing pressure seized her, forcing the precious air from her lungs. It was over. If she gave in to the urge to inhale, she'd die. . . .

The instinct to breathe overwhelmed her.

TEN

"That's a good girl. Spit it all up."

Coughing and gagging, she couldn't have spit if she wanted to—and she didn't want to. She wanted to breathe. Her lungs were stinging and her throat was on fire. She could taste bile in her mouth. She was sobbing. Her body was shaking uncontrollably. She was beyond the cold, further than the fear. She was in a place more unreal than death.

"Katherine, sweetheart, can you hear me? It's okay, baby. Just breathe. Slow and easy. It's okay. You're safe," she heard Peter say—and though it didn't seem to change anything, she believed him. She was safe. She could breathe. She was going to live.

He had her tipped to one side. She could feel his hands at her back, pushing her hair from her face, warming her legs and arms. He sounded frightened. She wanted to tell him that she loved him and how afraid she'd been when she thought she wouldn't have another chance to say so.

"What?" he asked. She could feel the warmth of his breath on her cheek. "Say it again, baby, I'm here."

"Sink. Like a rock."

"Thanks for the warning," he said, his profound relief escaping him in the form of a crazed chuckle. Exhausted, he moved over her body and collapsed on the deck beside her, uttering a wondrous "Jeezus."

While she relearned breathing, he clutched his chest and tried to convince himself he wasn't having a heart attack. Not that he didn't deserve one.

His heart had ceased to beat, and he knew he was dying as surely as she was when he'd first realized that she wasn't going to take his outstretched hand. He'd jumped into the water after her, and his heart hadn't started again until he'd grabbed her firmly around the waist. It had quit again when he knew she wasn't breathing and jumped when she coughed into his mouth and threw up on his leg. It came to a standstill once more when she wouldn't respond to him. He'd pinched her, and his chest filled with a pain greater than any he'd known before. When she began to cry, his heart sputtered back to life, beating too hard and too fast, aching with a gratitude that brought tears to his eyes.

He was fairly certain by now that his nearly forty-year-old heart wasn't in any kind of condition for this sort of stop-and-go exercise.

It wasn't until he could feel himself trembling, no

longer with fear but from the deep chilling cold in his bones, that he could look at Katherine again. She was blue and convulsing with cold, her knees drawn to her chest in an effort to warm herself.

"I'm going after blankets," he said, getting slowly to his feet. He wasn't sure if she could hear him, and he was pretty sure she didn't care where he was going, but he needed to put words in the air, to give the moment a sense of realness and normalcy. "I'll be right back. Don't go anywhere. And for crissake, stay away from the water."

He returned with a blanket and wrapped Katherine in the comforter from the wide bunk below. He picked her up and sat cradling her in his arms, holding her close, sharing what warmth he could muster.

"That was a stupid thing to do," he said, glancing down at her. Her eyes were closed. Her lips were blue, but she was breathing well enough. "Don't even think about ending any of our future arguments that way. I'm onto you now. Next time I'll let you drown."

She tried to tell him that she didn't ever again want to die, but all she got out was the last word.

"Very likely, but not today," he said. "My guess is that I'll end up strangling you someday. I'd be better off just throwing you back in the water now and getting it over with."

"No," she said, and in her mind she added a playful smile.

She missed the frown that came to Peter's face.

"I sure as hell hope you don't believe that stuff

about us messing with the boat," he said, continuing to talk for his own peace of mind as he searched the sea for help. "I have to be someone you trust."

"Cold."

"I know." He held her closer. "Just tell me you believe me."

"Can't ..." ... *get warm. I do ...* "believe you," she muttered, speaking aloud as many words as she could, her teeth chattering, her mind wandering in and out of darkness. "Can't lose ..." ... *you. You're too ...* "important to me."

If she'd opened her eyes, she'd have seen the hurt and bitterness in his eyes, the disappointment and scorn in the lines around his mouth. If she'd made the effort, she would have seen his jaw set with determination and his cheek ripple with anger.

Instead, she cuddled in the safety of his arms and let the heat of his body melt away the edges of her coldness. She was tired. Too tired to open her eyes to look at him. But then, she didn't really need to. His face was a clear picture in her heart, there to see whether her eyes were open or closed.

She fell asleep.

"Come in," she mouthed, motioning Quinn into her hospital room, then turning her attention back to the telephone conversation she was having.

"Not two minutes after I talked to Corrie," Jean was saying on the other end of the line, "Mr. Wesley called and wanted to know if his attorney was still here and could he speak with him."

"Which Mr. Wesley?" she asked.

"Uh, let's see . . ." There was a rustling of paper. "It was Peter Wesley that time, and then his brother, John, called later in the day."

Katherine's abdominal muscles ached with the slightest movement, and her throat was raw and hoarse—but those weren't the worst of the residual effects from her accident. She was missing time out of her life. Things had happened. People had done things. While she'd dozed off and on for nearly twenty-four hours, life had gone on without her.

Worst of all, she hadn't seen Peter since he'd kissed her good-bye at the hospital.

It seems the ship they'd signaled had seen their flares after all. She'd learned from a nurse that she'd been admitted to the hospital at about one thirty that afternoon, though she didn't remember any of the rescue, could barely recall Peter saying good-bye, and had vague in-and-out recollections of being moved, feeling overly warm, and telling her sisters to stop whispering over her body as if she were dead.

"Then what happened?" she asked Jean.

Jean relayed her story of breaking the news of the accident to Ted Evens and Mrs. Gumph and then went on to say that Mr. Bracken, attorney for the River Vista Project, returned to the room to smooth over any remaining unglued corners by generously offering them a wide berth and all the time they needed for her complete recovery and for the preparation of Belle's case.

"He said it nicely, but you could tell it went against his grain," she concluded, speaking of Robert Bracken.

Katherine glanced at the bright bouquet of flowers that arrived that morning from Belle, saying, "And what did Mrs. Gumph say to that?"

"Oh, she got huffy—you know how she does—and said that you'd have everything under control as soon as you were well and that you wouldn't be needing any of Mr. Wesley's charity."

She smiled at that. Under control? She hadn't had anything under control since she'd eaten dessert with John Wesley in Corrie's stead . . . actually, with Peter in Corrie's stead. Lord, what a mess it all was. She was beginning to wonder if she'd ever again know the feeling of being in control; if she'd ever really been in control; if there was such a thing as control.

"And what did the other Mr. Wesley want when he called?" she asked.

"Just to leave the message that his brother would be out of town for a few days and that if you should need to discuss any business, he would be available."

"Did he say where his brother was going?"

"Just out of town."

"Thanks, Jean. Anything else for me?" she asked, turning her mind to autopilot as she listened to messages, canceled appointments, and rescheduled meetings.

Her body felt heavy and confining. She felt small

and alone. Out Of Town was a big place. He might have gone to New York or Hong Kong. He could be in Timbuktu, Mali, or Walla Walla, Washington . . . or off the face of the earth, for all she knew.

He hadn't said anything about an upcoming trip. The chaste kiss on her forehead and the gentle stroking of her hair she remembered, wasn't what she would have called a going-out-of-town good-bye.

"Ah! Back from the dead again, I see," Corrie said, bursting into the room, tossing a box of her favorite coconut candies on her sister's lap. "You look almost as average as you ever did."

"I look," she said succinctly, "just like you."

"But I fix me up, so I look better than average."

"You look like a—"

"Spoon," Quinn said quickly, leaping to stand between them. "Always stirring things up."

"Yeah, well, she's got color in her cheeks again, so I can't be all bad," Corrie said, her attention catching on the box of candy she'd brought. "Mmm. My favorites. May I?"

"Help yourself," Katherine said, handing the box back to her. Then she smiled. "I guess it's the thought that counts." She watched Corrie take the box to the privacy of a chair in the corner before she asked, "Have you seen John Wesley lately?"

Corrie crossed her long legs and speared the cellophane on the box with a fingernail.

"Now, is that *seen* in the biblical sense, such as have I *seen* him naked and are we still sleeping together?"

she asked, knowing full well what was being asked of her. "Or is it a regular *seen*, like at the office where we discuss business, and do I know where Peter is?"

Katherine pretended to consider her options, then said, "Yes."

"Well then, yes, I do still see him in bed on occasion, but I caught him looking at Colleen's legs the other day, so I don't think I'll be seeing him there much longer." She was making a careful examination of her choice of chocolates. "Which, to be truthful, might be just as well. The sex is great. We're like two frontal storms meeting head-on, you know? But he's still the most obnoxious man I've ever had to do business with." She popped a chocolate-covered wad of sugared coconut into her mouth and looked up at her sisters.

She was a woman with information, and she liked having their attention. She had a talent for impregnating pauses, a gift really, and used it whenever she felt she could get away with it.

She chewed for a second or two, swallowed, and then, speaking like a squirrel with a nut in one cheek, she said, "I guess that brings us to the rest of the time I see John."

"Do you know where Peter is or not?" Quinn asked with impatience.

"No. All John will say is that he's out of town, and he'll be back in time for the court hearing."

"That's two weeks away," Katherine said. He left for two weeks without saying good-bye? Without a phone call or a note? That hurt. Like salt in a paper cut. "Well, good. I'll have all the more time to prepare Belle's case," she said, nursing her pride while tears stung at her eyes.

"And time to have lunch with me one day this week," Quinn added helpfully.

"You should get your hair done too," Corrie pointed out with a chocolate, before she ate it. Save Face was another game she was good at playing.

"The girls would love to see you," Quinn said. "They have this really cute duet they're working on with their piano teacher, and you know how they love a captive audience."

"Nordstrom's is having a huge sale you shouldn't miss."

"And Robert says he's found a great new used-book store he wants you to see."

"Sleep," Corrie said, concentrating harder on the candy than the game. "You'll actually be able to sleep now when you go to bed. You can eat peanut butter out of the jar with your finger. You can wear underpants with holes in them. You can draw little happy faces on the ends of the condoms in your medicine cabinet." She glanced up from the box of candy when the room went still. "What? What'd I say?"

Katherine succored a bruised ego and a severe heart condition for the better part of a week before her anger was strong enough to override the confusion and sadness and start demanding answers.

But of course, Peter wasn't there to give her any. He was somewhere, she knew, because every day he'd called his brother, who had then called Corrie to see how Katherine was doing. He had been checking on her, but even though John had confided that he was relaying information to Peter, he still wouldn't divulge his whereabouts.

So she filled her time at the law library and in the dusty archives of city hall, digging up statutes and reviewing zoning laws almost a century old. She also found documentation of the original purchase of the land on which the buildings stood, to one Herbert S. Albertson in the mid–seventeen hundreds. A remarkable find due to its age alone, but of little consequence to her case.

All the while she was filling her head with facts and figures—and her nose with dust—she was also building a personal arsenal of attack to use on Peter the next time she saw him.

She didn't have to turn around to know he had returned, where he was sitting in the courtroom, that he was somehow more handsome than she remembered, or that he was watching her—but she did.

Their gazes met and held and exchanged nothing. He was there. She was there. Whatever they were thinking or feeling toward each other they were at a Mexican standoff. Neither revealed the questions in their minds, the pain in their souls, the love in their hearts.

"You looking for me?"

Katherine jumped at the sound of the voice behind her and turned in her seat. Belle Gumph, weighed down in a mink shawl that had seen better days, and possibly every piece of expensive jewelry she owned, stood looking like a short but mighty queen ready to defend her territory.

"Were you afraid I was going to chicken out at the last minute?" she asked.

"It never crossed my mind," Katherine said, smiling. She'd developed a real fondness for the old lady over the past several months.

Belle looked around her. "Are you nervous?" she asked.

The question caught Katherine off guard. She was nervous. Nervous about the trial, though she'd tried bigger cases. And nervous about seeing Peter again, though she had their confrontation all worked out in her head, meticulously, in her usual manner.

"I want to do a good job for you, Belle," she said.

"Then let's get started."

There weren't many people in the courtroom. The usual officers, a few witnesses, two or three courthouse groupies. Few, aside from the participants, knew about the dispute. Even fewer cared whether or not Belle Gumph kept her buildings or that the homeless population would increase by at least twelve if she was forced to sell.

But Katherine cared. More than saving the last few tenants' homes, more than thumbing her nose in the face of the omnipotent attitude of the opposition, more even than the lofty issue of the individual's rights versus the majority's rule, she wanted to save Belle's memories.

Relatively speaking, the hearing was short. The judge, having received and reviewed copies of the depositions, circumvented most of the expert witnesses, calling only a few key attestants for clarification. He conceded to the buildings being in excellent condition for their age and commended Belle on her efforts—citing the fact that had all the property owners along River Street been as conscientious as she had been over the years, the need for the River Vista Project wouldn't exist.

His major concern, however, seemed to be relocating the tenants and, since the area was still zoned fifteen percent residential, how the city planned to meet the criteria once the last two buildings—Belle's—were torn down.

The city, with much ado, explained that lists of available housing had been given to all the tenants in Belle's buildings—to which the old woman jumped up and complained rather loudly that the spaces on the list were either miles away, too expensive, or death traps. It was then said that the city planners had designated a site a mere ten blocks from the project for low-income housing several years into the near future, to meet the present zoning law.

Belle and Katherine were nearly sick with disgust by the time the judge called a recess.

"I never heard such flimflamming garbage in all my born days," Belle grumbled, stomping out of the courtroom. "I got my house and a place in Florida to go to, but what are my people supposed to do? Pitch tents on the sidewalk until the city gets around to building them a place to live? There's not a thing wrong with either of those buildings. Solid as rock and not a bug or a mouse between 'em. There's no reason to pull them down."

"I know, Belle," Katherine said quietly, feeling as if all her time and effort were no more than beach sand, slipping through her fingers without worth, making no impression where it fell. "We'll get one more stab at it in our summation, then we'll have to wait and see. Are you hungry? Shall we go have lunch?"

Belle hesitated, then shook her old gray head. "You run along. I'll meet you back here at one."

"Where are you going?"

"I got things to do," she said, already walking away.

Katherine had things to do, too, she just didn't know what to do first.

It wasn't long, however, before a reasonable order presented itself. She spotted the Wesley brothers conversing with their attorney and several city officials across from the elevators and decided to start at the top of her list.

Could she simply march up to Peter and demand an explanation, the way she'd planned it in her head? Being a triplet had nothing to do with the fact that she had three times the pride of most women—or three times the cowardice. She just couldn't bring herself to challenge him head-on. Instead, she decided to play his game. Snub him. Pretend that his presence within a fifty-mile diameter of her didn't phase her in the least. Not an easy pretense.

"Mr. Bracken," she responded coolly when the lawyer looked up, smiled, and greeted her with a nod. When John and Peter, with eyes identical in color but worlds apart in expression, met her gaze, she used the same tone when she inclined her head to them.

She stood at the elevators with her back to them, waiting. It was Peter's place to approach her. He was the one with the answers; all she had were questions. He was the one who'd left town. This was all his fault. She'd been sitting there like a dumb lump for weeks, waiting for him to return. Waiting.

Or was it all his fault? Her anger faltered. What if she was to blame? What if she'd said or done something. . . . No, not this time. This time it was him, his doing, his fault.

The elevator doors opened and she walked in. She stood stick stiff waiting for the doors to close.

Waiting. Why was she always the one waiting? she asked herself, instantly furious when she noticed that he'd returned to the conversation as if he hadn't seen her, as if he had nothing to say to her, as if she meant nothing to him. Worst of all, as if he meant nothing to her!

Something inside snapped and she heard a growl,

as if a wild animal were suddenly afoot. She brushed past a couple who'd followed her into the elevator, then pounced.

"I'd like to speak with you," she said, looking directly at Peter.

He turned his head slowly and looked at her dispassionately.

So beautiful, he thought, steeling himself against the flashing lights of high emotions in her eyes. She was angry, inflamed, frightened . . . and, damn her, wary of him. He was tempted to snatch her into his arms, kiss her, stroke her, play her like a fine violin until she sang out in ecstasy and surrendered to him. Totally.

He could do that, had done it on more than one occasion. But it wasn't enough. Not anymore. It wasn't enough to hold her trembling, bowed, and begging beneath him. It wasn't enough to see her eyes glaze over with need, to hear her whisper his name, to cuddle with her in the dark. He wanted more.

He wanted her to believe in him; to know that if she fell, he'd catch her. He wanted her to feel free to have her own opinions, to act on them and to trust that he wouldn't interfere. He wanted her to have faith in him, to count on him, to realize that watching her in all her gentle righteousness and strength of intelligence was his greatest pleasure. He wanted her to know these things in her mind, feel them in her heart, in her soul.

But she didn't, and that hurt.

"So speak," he said rudely.

"In private."

"Isn't it a little late to be settling this out of court?"

"This isn't about the buildings. It's personal."

His brows lifted, as if he were surprised.

"Personal?" He looked as if he were about to deny that they had anything personal to say to each other, but John's elbow in his ribs and his scornful frown seemed to change his mind. "Okay. Where?"

She looked around hastily. There was an urgency building up inside her like steam in a teakettle.

Noon didn't automatically mean lunch to everyone in the courthouse. The halls were crowded and bustling. Women were running in and out of the rest room as if someone were passing out free boxes of chocolate inside, and though she couldn't imagine what they'd be serving in the men's room, it was equally as busy. The isolated conference rooms were on the other end of the building.

"Here," he said, walking casually over to a utility closet, opening the door, and waving her in. He glanced over his shoulder at his companions and said, "If I'm not back in a couple of days, tell Mom I loved her."

ELEVEN

"You think this is funny?" she asked, turning and attacking immediately. All the basic rules of good communication flew out the window. The techniques for proper and efficient verbal examination of a witness were flushed down the toilet of human nature. She was mad and she hurt and she wanted some answers. "Do you think you're so charming and handsome that you can go off for two weeks without a word and then come back expecting me to throw myself at you and welcome you back? Where the hell have you been and why didn't you say good-bye?"

"I went home," he said, crossing his arms defensively in front of him, carefully posturing a shoulder against the wall. He wanted to kiss her so bad, he could taste it. But he was vying for more than a kiss here, and he needed to keep his thoughts straight. "I went to Milwaukee."

Still furious, she opened and closed her mouth in confusion.

"To see your mother?"

"Partly." Mostly he'd gone to get away, to clear his mind and straighten his thoughts. It had been a useless trip. He was no more sure now than he had been when he'd left of how to handle her, how to make her trust him, how to convince her that the doubts and suspicions she had were generated from her own guilts, her own insecurities. He was in no way prepared for a confrontation. Nevertheless, he would do the best he could.

"You couldn't have told me you were going to see your mother? Doesn't your mother have a phone? Couldn't you have called me, just once, to tell me where you were? You didn't even say good-bye."

"I said good-bye. At the hospital," he said shortly. "You look well, by the way."

"No thanks to you," she said, then paused. "Well, I guess it is because of you, but . . . but what if I'd taken a sudden turn for the worse? I didn't know where you were or how long it would take you to get back. What if I'd needed you?"

"Did you need me?"

It was on her lips to say no, she hadn't needed him. But they weren't talking physical now.

"Yes, I did. I did need you."

"What for?"

She frowned. "To . . . talk to. To be with. I . . ." Frustrated, she reverted back to anger. "What the hell is this? A game? I thought we had something special together. You said you loved me."

"And I meant it."

"Then what's happened? What have I done?"

For a moment he seemed to turn into a block of cold, hard stone, then suddenly he exploded, shattering his steely shroud of indifference.

"Not *done*. Do!" he shouted, the energy in him so forceful and so poorly contained that it seemed to push him away from the wall and shoot out through the wild movements of his hands. He felt an urge to shake her till her head rattled—then he caught the tail of his anger and held on tight.

He jammed his hands into his pockets and spoke again in a diminished volume.

"Can't anything just *happen*, without it being someone's fault?" he asked. "Is everything and everyone you touch, *your* responsibility? I'd like to know, Katherine. I need to know if I fell in love with a woman who thinks she's God or if she's some poor fool who thinks the earth gravitates on an axis because of what she does and what she thinks."

She folded her arms across her midsection because it was tight and aching. She straightened her spine to feel taller, bigger, stronger, as the walls closed in around her.

"We came in here to talk, Katherine. So talk. Fight back."

"I would if I knew what the hell you were talking about."

"I'm talking about you. I'm talking about the way you came in here all steamed up, then backed off and asked what you'd done," he said, his temper building again. "I'm talking about the way you take everyone else's problems and make them your own. I'm talking about . . . about that crazy knight and the fat guy . . ." he said, so provoked that he lost his train of thought for a second.

"The . . . what?"

"That story you loved as a kid. *Don Quixote.* My mother had a copy and I reread it. He lives in a fantasyland of truth and beauty and idealism, and when he can't make everything as perfect as he thinks it should be, he feels guilty and blames himself. The guy dies thinking he's a failure, for crissake."

She frowned. Her eyes narrowed suspiciously.

"Are you saying that you think I'm crazy? That I live in a fantasyland?"

"No. I'm saying you're an idealist who takes all the blame when she can't make everything as perfect as she thinks it should be."

"There's nothing wrong with trying to make the world a better place to live in."

"There's nothing wrong with trying, but there's something very wrong with taking all the responsibility and feeling all the guilt and giving up the happiness in your own life when you fail."

His guard was thinning to a point where she could almost see that he was suffering too. Or was it her imagination that colored his dark eyes with disillusionment and sorrow? Obviously, she'd missed a lot more than she'd thought during the accident.

"I don't do that," she said, attempting to understand his thinking.

"Like hell. You do it with your sisters all the time."

"I don't feel responsible for my sisters' happiness."

"No? Then what about the switch? You said you hated doing it. You said you felt guilty for doing it. But how would you have felt if you'd refused to help Corrie out?" She didn't answer. "My guess is that you'd have felt more guilt *not* helping her than you did pulling the switch. For you it was the lesser of two evils. A little guilt or a lot of guilt."

"She's my sister," she said, as if that were reason enough for nearly anything she might do. But in this case he was right. She'd sacrificed her peace of mind, acted against her usual standards of honesty and good faith, and let projected guilt lead her into an act that she knew was wrong. "I didn't think it would get as complicated as it did. I didn't think anyone would be hurt."

"Except yourself?"

"I'd done it before. It was something I knew I could live with."

"Okay. You wanted your sisters to be happy with their music and sports when you were kids. So you gave up your reading time, your alone time, your thinking time, and subjected yourself to failure upon failure for them."

That she was tone-deaf and clumsy weren't truths

she'd needed to take classes to learn, she thought. But what kid grew up without a few embarrassing moments and a couple of humiliating self-discoveries to reckon with?

"Did you ever once tell your parents to leave you alone, that all you really wanted to do was read and walk in the woods?"

She tried to remember.

"No."

"Why not?"

"I don't know."

"Afraid you'd disappoint them? Maybe you weren't sure how they'd react. Did you think they'd hold the other two back because of you? Couldn't you have asked for your share to come in the form of books?"

"We . . ." She stopped herself. Books were a shared thing. She'd borrowed most of those she'd read from the library, because the books at home were . . . Nancy Drew came to mind, and she felt an instant and irrational irritation. "That was a long time ago. I can't remember if that was an option for me or not."

It was killing him to hurt her, but if it was the only way to get her to act on her emotions instead of her thoughts, he had to keep trying.

"All right. Let's try this one. You've set yourself up as a defender of the rights of the individual—underdog actually. A noble cause. Certainly fertile territory for an idealist, or even someone who's had a lot of practice at doing for others what she can't do for herself without feeling guilty about it."

"Such as?" she asked tersely.

"Grabbing her own happiness." Her angry eyes shifted a bit, as if she might be looking for the tiniest thread of truth in his words. He forged ahead. "But at least as the spokesperson for the downtrodden, you can think that what you do and say is truer and more valid than your opposition. And if you win, then of course you were right all along. But if you lose, then something has to be wrong. Something in the system, maybe. You go back. You retrace your steps, rework your case, go over and over it because you grew up thinking that all things must be equal, the world must be fair to everyone."

He took several steps toward her, watching her intently.

"The trouble is, you can't find anything wrong. You haven't overlooked anything. So, who's to blame then? Who's left?" He stepped closer. "You're the human factor, Katherine. You're the flaw. But, hey, you've always been able to make the fairness system work, haven't you? All you've ever had to do is give up a little of your own pleasure, forfeit a little of your own happiness, suffer a few hardships. Maybe you didn't explain something well enough this time. Maybe you didn't fight hard enough. Maybe you let someone influence you."

"That's not true," she said, even as she recognized the design of her nature. "At least, I don't mean to . . . I mean, I don't really think those things."

"Are you saying that your appeal is going so well

that you didn't mean to accuse me and then my brother of sabotaging the boat so you'd miss that damn deposition?" he asked, his pain now raw and exposed. "You didn't mean to imply that we're dirty and underhanded enough to resort to trickery and manipulation of the law to get what we want? You don't really think so little of me that I had to persuade you to believe that I wouldn't endanger a bunch of helpless old people for the sake of something built of steel and concrete?" He paused to take a breath. "I'm pretty easygoing for the most part, but don't for a minute assume that I'm stupid, Katherine."

He couldn't stop his hands from reaching for her. His anger was nothing compared to his love for her. He wanted so badly to hold her, to give back all she had given away.

"Only a fool would have missed the pattern in your thinking," he went on. "And I'm no fool. I wasn't about to hang around until you worked your way up to the presumption that the only reason I was with you was to control this trial." He turned from her suddenly, as if he couldn't finish what he had to say, standing so close to her. "Hell, I'd get sick inside every time you brought up that conflict-of-interest crap. I didn't know why at first, but I know now." He absently rubbed at the knots of tension at the back of his neck. "I was scared. More scared than I ever thought I could be, more than I ever want to be again. Know why?"

Stunned, she shook her head. He stepped close again, bending his face to hers.

"Because deep inside I knew that if push ever came to shove, you'd pick this damn trial over me. Whether I influenced you or not, it wouldn't matter. If you lost this case, it would mean the world is unfair, and that's not possible. So you'd take the blame, and your guilt would lead you directly to your relationship with me. You'd choose your guilt over my love."

He waited for her to deny his fears, and when she stood staring at him, he said, "Say something, Katherine. Call me crazy."

Of course he was crazy. They both knew he was crazy. And she had plenty to say. She did. She just couldn't think of the words. Words. Lord, how many words had she read in her lifetime? How many places had they taken her to? How many ideas had they explained to her? How many pictures had they painted for her? Words were her livelihood. Where were they now?

Peter released a resigned sigh and stepped away from her. "Okay. So I'm not crazy," he said.

"Peter," she said, her voice a tight-sounding croak.

He shook his head and held up his hand to stop her.

"It's okay, Katherine. Some things last a lot longer than our love affair, but nothing lasts forever."

"Some things do. Peter. Please. Wait. Give me a minute to think. I don't know what to say, except that you're wrong about me. I love you. And . . . and I wouldn't . . . I wasn't . . ."

"Katherine," he said quietly, his anger spent, his

soul heavy with sadness. "Forget it. You don't need to bust a blood vessel over this. You shouldn't have to think about it. What I wanted from you should have come naturally, from your gut. I admit we started out in a mutual deception, but I also thought we'd started over on even ground after that. I didn't tamper with the boat, and I haven't given you cause to distrust me since the first time we made love. At least, not that I know of—and please, feel free to correct me if you can." He paused to give her a chance to speak and to take in some much-needed air. "You might not have meant what you said on the boat the other day. But I think your imagination was working on it, looking for some reason to distrust me, like a safety net in case you lost this case. Loving me would be an easy scapegoat for your guilt."

He turned to leave. With his hand on the knob and his face to the door, he stopped. He bowed his head and was quiet for a moment.

Her nerves were wound tighter than the springs in a cheap clock. Was he reconsidering his words? Was he changing his mind? Was he giving her another chance to speak? Her mind ran amok.

"I don't suppose it'll make any difference, but I think you're a damned fine lawyer. You haven't missed anything; you haven't done anything wrong. You put up a good fight. I haven't seen better. You're still going to lose, but that happens sometimes. Maybe with me out of the way, you'll be able to get a clearer picture of that."

He closed the door softly, but the impact shattered her heart into a hundred pieces. Her insides shriveled and twisted. She wrapped her arms about her waist to contain the pain, forcing her every breath. There wasn't a thought in her head, except that Peter was gone—and even that didn't seem real. Or maybe it was too real to comprehend? Too true to deal with?

All that was her world focused on the pain, wandered about in the numbness, reeled in time. There was no telling how long she stood among the mops and chemical cleaners in a mental void. She vacillated from disbelief to denial to cautiously considering Peter's words as truth.

How rigid was she? How weak was her capacity to love? Had the idea that John might have meddled with the boat been more than a flash in an overheated pan of panic? Was she in the habit of thinking herself a martyr to the will of those she loved? Had she disapproved of Peter's business practices in particular or business practices in general? When she told Belle about her personal relationship with Peter, what if she had been forced to choose between them? Had she done her best for Belle? Had she let Peter's interests influence her at all? Had she ever once considered what would have happened between them if she won Belle's appeal? Would Peter have loved her less? Did that thought ever once cross her mind?

She left the utility closet, feeling shaken to the core, and without any answers. She blinked at the sights before her, lost and disoriented.

The familiar halls of the courthouse were somehow different to her. Everything had changed in some way. The woodwork was darker and more detailed. The marble floors looked as slick and dangerous as wet glass. The faces of people she might not have taken notice of before took on clarity and definition, each with its own story and emotions.

Before her eyes life converted from black and white to vivid Technicolor. It was blinding. It gave her a headache. It turned the rest of the afternoon into a kaleidoscope of brilliant failures and bright disappointments with an array of psychedelic ramifications—including intense guilt.

Peter had been right. The appeal to save Belle's buildings from destruction was denied. The judge set what he thought to be a fair selling price and ordered Belle to take it. Then he gave her twenty-one days to evacuate.

"I'm sorry, Belle," she said, doing what came naturally—taking blame and feeling guilty. Already, she was reviewing her preparation before the hearing, her summation, her briefs. "I'm really sorry."

"Well, you win some and lose some. That's life," the old lady said, as if the loss of her buildings were one more thing to get over and go on without. "We gave it our best. It was a long shot, I grant you, but we took it. That's what counts."

That's what counts? Taking the shot whether you

win or lose? Frankly, Katherine liked to win, no matter what. Losing was failure and failure was . . .

Peter was right. She couldn't accept failure, not as anything but a personal affront. A humiliation. An insult to her self-respect. Already she could feel her pride warring to overcome it, to make it right, to find an excuse for it.

Without intention, she turned in her chair and looked back at Peter. He sat watching her, as if waiting to see what she'd do or if she'd say something.

There was no I-told-you-so in his expression. It was worse than that. She saw sadness and pity.

He watched as her gaze lowered away from his in shame. If he didn't have so much at stake, he'd have grabbed her in his arms and taken all her doubts and self-castigation into his own heart. But it would have been like trying to catch fog in a jar or a dream in a box. For as real as her suffering was, its source was false and deceptive. A fallacy. A distorted reflection that only Katherine could correct.

"Well, young man," Belle said, stopping beside him on her way out, Katherine directly behind her. "I don't suppose it'll do any good to ask you to tear them down gently."

His smile was sympathetic and kind.

"I'll do what I can, Mrs. Gumph."

"Sure, sure. You know, despite our differences, you're not such a bad boy. Now, the other one"—she motioned with her thumb toward John—"he reminds me of my Darwood, God love him. That same drive.

The blind ambition. He'd send the wrecking ball in on my buildings without blinking an eye, but you . . . you'll at least cover the damn thing in velvet before you let 're go."

"You're quite a lady, Mrs. Gumph. I wish we'd met under happier circumstances."

"Well, don't let this little bit of business hold you back, boy. Call me, Belle—whenever you want to."

Little bit of business? Katherine's inner turmoil wouldn't allow her to speak. She couldn't rely on her emotions, much less her mouth.

"Thank you. I will," he said, and then, more for his own curiosity than Katherine's conscience, he observed, "You know, you're taking this much better than I thought you would."

"I can afford to," she said brightly. This time she aimed her thumb in her attorney's direction and said, "This one feels bad enough for both of us."

His brows rose in surprise. So, he wasn't the only one who knew about Katherine's overactive scruples. Their eyes met over the old woman's head.

"I'm sure she does," he said.

One minute she wanted to tear at Peter's face with her claws out. The next minute she wanted to be invisible. The next, she was tempted to cry and blubber all over his shirtfront, begging for forgiveness. And then a sense of self-righteousness would surge through her, insisting she had nothing to be sorry for.

"That's why I keep her on board," Belle was saying. "She can't stand to lose, so she works harder than most.

She never loses, unless it was a hopeless case to begin with."

"Losing is a relative thing sometimes, don't you think?" he asked, holding Katherine's gaze a moment longer before he shifted his to Belle. "Aren't there times when you can win more by losing, and other times when you can lose everything by winning?"

Belle put wrinkles in her wrinkles as she narrowed her eyes to study him, then craned her neck to examine Katherine intently.

"*Everything* is relative, boy," she said, her wise old eyes lingering on the young attorney before she turned back to him. "But you don't live as long as I have without figuring out that life is one big boat, and we're all in it. Everybody's doing the best they can with what they got, and us that have plenty to work with shouldn't judge or look unkindly on those who have less."

Tolerance wasn't a virtue Katherine would have attributed to Belle Gumph, but at the moment it was as accurate as everything else she was thinking and feeling.

Even before she followed Belle out of the courtroom, she could feel her systems overloading and shutting down. She missed the amenities exchanged between Peter and Belle. When he looked at her, sharp and searching, and he moved his lips, she heard nothing but the roar of the vacuum inside her.

Walking came automatically, but she couldn't feel the floor beneath her. The late afternoon sun was bright, but she couldn't feel its warmth. Life went on for several more days, but she couldn't distinguish one moment from the next.

She hid herself from the world by spending long hours in her office, staying well after the firm's doors were locked for the night. She shuffled papers she couldn't concentrate on, rearranged files on her desk as if there were some sort of logic in it. More often than not, however, she would simply lean back in her chair to study the stipple pattern on the ceiling.

Her thoughts turned inward, looking for answers to questions she didn't wholly understand. Was guilt a prime motivational factor in her life? And if it was, was that so horrible? Was it worse than being motivated by greed or power?

In the parking garage she disengaged the security system on her car and then for no reason she knew, reengaged it and took the stairs to the street above.

She was blocks away before she realized she should have left her briefcase behind—not that she knew where she was going.

But the night was cool and clear. A gentle breeze, coming from the river and the ocean beyond, seemed to be taking all the heat from the turmoil in her mind. It blew her thoughts away, one by one, as she gave herself up to the aimlessness of her walking and indulged herself with the numbness inside her.

"Katherine?"

She stopped, but it took her a second or two to figure out why. She turned. She was as startled to see

John Wesley leaving one of Belle Gumph's buildings
as she was to discover where her feet had taken her.

"John?"

"Good guess," he said, descending the steps with
a grace very much like his brother's. "Or are you
that good at telling us apart that you can do it in
the dark too?"

"I'm that good," she said, unaccountably glad to
see him. For some reason she took a sort of comfort
in John's presence. "But it was extra easy this time.
Peter wouldn't have noticed me."

He smiled and chuckled indulgently.

"He'd have noticed."

His words were like a reassuring pat on the back,
but not an open invitation to discuss her personal
problems with his brother. Not that Katherine would
have known how to talk about it anyway. Arguing was
her profession, but even a novice needed a fundamental
understanding of the basic issue at hand. At present her
hands were empty.

"What are you doing down here?" she asked, looking around asking herself the same question.

"I had a couple of things to look in on," he said,
nodding toward the construction site further down the
street. "And Peter wanted me to check in with the old
lady to see if she needed any help moving out. Labor.
Vans. That sort of thing."

She nodded, knowing immediately that it hadn't
been a nose-rubbing offer.

"That's nice. I'm sure Belle appreciates it."

"I couldn't find her. I'm pretty sure that's her car," he said, his gaze shifting to a shiny black town car parked across the street. "But she didn't answer her door."

"Do you think something's wrong?" she asked, instantly worried.

"No. I could hear the TV through the door. She probably saw me coming."

Katherine continued to frown. Belle had been resigned after the hearing, not angry.

"She might not have heard me," John added as another possibility. "The TV was pretty loud."

Maybe Belle's hearing impairment was more than a social convenience after all?

"Well, I was on my way to see her myself," she said impulsively. "If I can get her to answer the door, I'll tell her about your offer."

"Good. Thanks," he said, as they began to step away from each other. "Have her call the office and . . . just tell us what she needs."

"I will. And thanks, John."

"No problem," he said with a casual wave as he stepped off the curb, walking down the street to his car. "See ya."

"See ya," she murmured in return, wondering if she would. She turned and walked up the steps to Belle's door.

"Katherine?" John called.

"Yes?"

"He'd have noticed."

She nodded her understanding, then slipped inside the building. Peter might have noticed her wandering about on the streets, but would he have spoken to her? she wondered, glancing at the marked and remarked labels on the mailboxes at the bottom of the stairs.

She was halfway up the first flight of steps, pondering what might have happened had she met Peter instead of John moments earlier, when she heard a crashing noise coming from somewhere below her.

Looking over the banister, she saw nothing, but heard another rumbling and thumping of disaster accompanied by a few colorful curses.

"Belle?"

She retraced her steps and followed the clattering sounds to the rear of the building, where she found a door ajar and a set of steps leading to the basement of the building.

"Belle?" she called down the well, certain of the foghorn voice she was hearing. "Hello?"

"Who is it?" came gruffly. Belle appeared at the bottom of the stairs with a baseball bat in her hands. "Who's up there?"

"It's me, Belle. Katherine." The old woman squinted up at her. "What are you doing down there?"

The bat came down to her side while she placed the other fist on her hip, cocked her head, and said, "I'm hosting a batting practice. What do you think I'm doing?"

"Well, I don't know," she said, taking the concrete steps carefully. If they were as old as the smell emanating from that general direction, they couldn't be safe. "It sounds as if you're having a war down here."

"That's a thought," she said, turning and disappearing into the gloom. "I oughta just blow the place up," she muttered through the sound of collapsing boxes. "Save me a lot of time and trouble."

Katherine stood at the bottom of the stairs and offered a small prayer that Mr. Robanichek was as good an exterminator as he'd said he was, because if *she* were a river rat looking for a safe place to hide, the boxes piled six and seven high, the chairs, lamps, knickknacks, and several hundred tons of other miscellaneous paraphernalia crammed into the basement of Belle's building, would have been her first choice.

"Holly cow," she murmured, scanning the stash. "I thought my parents were pack rats, but this is . . . this is . . ."

"Pretty amazing, huh?"

"Amazing. Yes." Belle had her head in a box, digging deep as if looking for something specific. "What are you going to do with all this junk?"

"Junk?" Belle stood up and looked around. "This stuff isn't junk. This is a gold mine. My gold mine."

Katherine felt as if she'd walked from a bad dream into a nightmare. Cautiously she lifted the flap of a nearby box to peer in at dusty kitchen utensils.

"I think you should go with your blow-the-place-up idea," she said, wrinkling her nose in .sgust. A thought hit her. "Good Lord, Belle, you're not think-ing of moving all this stuff, are you?"

Belle looked around as if she might have wanted to take it all with her. "No. I'll take some of it, of course, but I have a young fella coming tomorrow to buy most of it," she said.

"Buy it?"

"Antiques, dear girl. People pay good money for jun—things like this," she said, picking up a large ceramic vase. "Memorabilia is very in these days, you know."

Memorabilia. Katherine watched as Belle turned the vase over in her hands, looking at it as if it were a treasure from the past, as if it had once belonged to a czar, as if wars had been fought over it. Memorabilia. Cherished riches from Belle's past.

A familiar sensation surged through her, like blood, but darker and without any life-giving force. Guilt came to call like an old friend who was neither liked nor welcomed. She felt herself taking it in, like something physical, because it was her habit to do so; because it was well-known to her; because . . . because when she needed to feel something and invited her emotions to gather about her, guilt—like the guest from hell—always arrived first, ate everything that wasn't nailed down, drank everything that poured, was the loudest and most obnoxious visitor and always left last.

"Maybe . . . you could store it all someplace," she said, her heart aching with the thought of Belle parting with her sentimental possessions. "I . . . I was just talking to John Wesley. He'd like to donate manpower and transportation to help you move. We could make him sorry he offered," she said, smiling, hoping to appeal to Belle's sense of humor.

"That we could do," she agreed, chuckling softly. She took stock of her surroundings, then looked at Katherine. "But it's time to move on."

Katherine had to look away. The sadness in the old woman's voice tore at her heart. Seeing someone like Belle Gumph defeated and submissive was more than she could bear. That she had had a hand in bringing her to this point was shaming.

"Okay," Belle said authoritatively. "What's going on here? You didn't come all the way down here to tell me the Wesley boys wanted to help me move, did you?"

"Uh, no. I . . . uh, was in the neighborhood."

"*This* neighborhood? Doing what?"

"Uh . . . walking." She pointed above ground. "I saw John Wesley upstairs. Out front. He, uh, I was worried about you when he told me he couldn't get you to answer your door. Upstairs."

Belle cackled with glee.

"So, you thought I was so depressed I was up there slitting my wrists over this, huh?"

"No, of course not. I was just worried."

Belle's eyes were old but keen and astute.

"You're a sweet girl, but if I was you, I'd worry more about myself than some old woman who won't thank you for fretting over her."

"I'm not looking for any thanks."

"What are you looking for? Absolution?"

"Absolution? For what?"

"That's what I want to know," Belle said. She stepped around a pile of boxes and came closer to get a better look at Katherine's face. "You're beating yourself up about something. What else have you screwed up besides my hearing?"

"I didn't screw up your hearing," she said, defensive and angry.

"Well, I didn't think so, but you're feeling bad about something." She turned to rummage through another filthy box of odds and ends. "Must be the fight you had with your young man."

"How did you know about that?"

"The first time I heard about it was from the man at the newsstand in the lobby of the courthouse. I got all the details in the ladies' room on the third floor," she said without looking up. "They musta forgot to put a soundproof door on the janitor's broom closet."

Katherine groaned and gave up. She sat down on the concrete step and buried her face in her hands. She didn't care if her best blue silk suit got snagged and stained. She didn't care if a herd of rats scurried across her back. She didn't care if she choked to death on dust that was older than she was. She didn't care . . .

"Personally," Belle went on, "I don't believe things I hear in ladies' rooms. You may be young and you may not know junk from priceless antiques, but I'm a pretty good judge of character and I don't think you'd let guilt rule your life. You're not a selfish person."

Guilt, she knew. But how did it connect with being selfish? Her brand of remorse had her doing any number of things she didn't really want to do. How could that be selfish? She lowered her hands and let them fall between her knees as she watched Belle rummage through her boxes.

"Taking the blame and feeling guilty about everything can be real tricky sometimes," Belle was saying. "A little bit is healthy—keeps folks on the straight and narrow, you know? But too much guilt can be very dangerous."

"Dangerous?"

"Sure. When you take responsibility for everything that happens, you make yourself the center of everything. It's selfish and egotistical. You start to think that what you do or don't do can control everything that goes on around you. You start thinking, if I don't do this, such and such will happen; or because I did this, such and such will happen. Then you start thinking you can control people, too, which I think is actually sort of stupid because everyone knows you can't control what other people think and do, much less what they'll think or do in a specific situation."

She stood up and pondered the subject for a moment, then moved to another box. "I don't have children, but I could never figure out why parents feel guilty or responsible for what their kids think and do and say . . . unless it's to keep the kids from growing up and taking responsibility for their own actions and thoughts and words, as if they could actually control the kids' minds or something.

"Anyway, I wouldn't hire a lawyer who thought she could control what happens in my life." She laughed. "I can't control my life. Can you imagine what a pompous pea-head someone like that would be?"

She was beginning to, yes.

"Well, what if the lawyer's intentions were good?" Katherine asked. "I mean, what if she didn't think of it as trying to control everything, but of doing what she thought was right or . . . what she thought was a kind thing to do or a favor for someone or . . . well, what if she had good reasons for the things she did and the way she felt?"

"That's selfish too."

"Why?"

"Letting someone else deal with their own problems, make their own mistakes, and live their own life can be painful to watch—especially to someone who thinks they can control everything. They feel responsible for other people's happiness, so they make up good reasons to step in and live someone else's life for them or at the very least show them how to do it better. But then we're back to trying to control life, which can't be done. Ah-ha! Here we are," she exclaimed suddenly, all but dancing a jig as she tugged and pulled at a particular box stacked amid the heaps of boxes.

"Belle!" she cried, getting to her feet. "Careful. You'll get buried in all that stuff if you're not—"

The wall of cartons came tumbling down as Belle pulled the box free and bustled out of harm's way.

"Careful," Katherine finished needlessly. Despite her newfound fondness for the old woman, she had a feeling that Belle Gumph would be the death of her yet.

"I'd have stayed here till I starved to death before I left this box behind," Belle said, setting it down ceremoniously on another pile of junk. "Do you know what's in here?"

Did she care?

"Uh, Belle? Before you tell me what's in the box, would you answer one question for me?"

"Sure." She was peeling tape away and prying the box open.

"Well, say someone did have, say, more guilt than they ought to have sometimes. How . . . I mean, how would they go about getting rid of it?"

Belle looked her straight in the eye and smiled kindly.

"Accept the fact that you're human. Forgive yourself for making mistakes. Forget and move on." She waited two seconds for this to sink in, then . . . moved on.

"Have you ever read Joshua H. Albertson?" she asked. "No? He is, without a doubt, the least-recognized poetic genius since . . . well, of all time, I think. And he's wonderful. If it were up to me, he'd be mandatory reading in every high school in this country."

"His name is familiar."

"My favorite is 'Riverbank: When the Water Goes to Sea.' He wrote it when he was just seventeen, standing no more than a thousand feet from this very spot."

TWELVE

Katherine smothered a huge yawn. She was dead-on-her-feet exhausted, and bursting with energy. A night with Belle Gumph could do that to a person, she supposed, smiling.

The elevator lifted, startling the butterflies in her stomach. She breathed deeply, filling her lungs with air and her spirit with a sense of well-being. For the first time in days since her baptism in the sea—no, since she first met Peter—no, before that . . .

Well, anyway, for the first time in a long time, Katherine felt like Katherine—only better. For the first time, maybe, in her entire life, she felt she knew herself. Who she was. Why she did the things she did. Why she felt the way she felt.

She was a woman full of flaws, and that was okay. In fact, it was great.

The elevator doors opened onto the airy, glass-enclosed offices occupied by the Safran River Vista

Project Planners—namely John and Peter Wesley.

She stepped out with a full head of steam and kept on going. Nothing and no one could stop her now. She was Katherine Asher, and she could be wrong about certain things—but this time she wasn't.

The receptionist stood and tried to flag her down with her arms. "Excuse me. Can I help you?" she called as Katherine passed her desk.

"I don't think so."

A secretary offered her kind assistance as well, in a rather loud, commanding voice. She simply smiled at her as she pushed her way through the door into the spacious corner office.

"I'm here to make a deal," she announced, even before the two unsuspecting brothers looked up. They'd had their heads together over a stack of papers and hadn't seen her coming. "But first I want to apologize."

"That sounds like my cue to leave," John said, taking two steps toward the door before she stopped him.

"No. Please don't. This involves you both," she said, her gaze meeting Peter's. She'd missed him, more than she'd realized. His presence in the room was a comfort and a contest at once. She felt safe and secure, as if she'd finally come home, and yet she knew a need to seek his approval, to win his acceptance, and to earn his love.

"I . . . I may not have meant it at the time I said it, but I did accuse you both of some pretty rotten things, and I think you might have been right," she said, her eyes lowering and then lifting back to Peter's. "I think those thoughts might have kept coming back and coming back, and sounding more and more reasonable to me after I lost the appeal. I think eventually I might have convinced myself that you were both capable of underhanded business practices and of manipulating the law—and me. And so, for that seed of what might have been, I apologize to you. To both of you."

When it became apparent that they didn't know how to respond to this sort of left-handed confession, she continued. She still had plenty to say.

"However, I won't apologize to you, to either of you, for anything else," she said, setting her briefcase down on one of the two large desks in the office. "I make mistakes. I don't have all the answers. Hell, I don't even know all the questions, but if this is something I have to learn to accept about myself, then the rest of the world is going to have to accept it too."

Emotionally, this turf was a little shaky for her. Perhaps it was time to go professional, where she stood on terra firma.

"I do know one thing for sure, though," she said. "I am a damn fine lawyer. And I'm here to make you one very solid and unbreakable promise."

"Which is?" John asked cautiously—as Peter seemed to be a bit far out in left field to notice that she had that certain life-and-happiness-as-you-know-it-is-now-legally-over look in her eyes that always struck fear into the breasts of even the most hard-core businessmen.

She raised her right hand and formally vowed, "I will make your lives a living nightmare if you don't find some way to incorporate Belle Gumph's buildings into the River Vista Project."

"For crissake!" bellowed John as he threw his arms up to the world in total frustration. "What is the matter with you? Are you stupid or just stubborn?" He didn't want to insult her but, dammit, she was like a summer cold he couldn't get rid of. "This was all settled over two weeks ago. We have quad-copies of the documents stating that we won fair and square, and that those buildings are to come down. I have a copy here, as a matter of fact." He began to riffle through the papers on his desk. "Which part don't you understand? We can read it together. I'll explain it as we go."

"I don't think that's the problem," Peter said, watching Katherine expectantly, keenly sensing something new and unexplored in her.

"Then what the hell is it?"

"History," she said, her voice soft, her smile pleased.

"History?" John knew history; he had a history with the Asher sisters. One was as clever as she was ditzy, one was as talented as she was good-natured, and one was as clever and talented as the other two put together—plus smart. John didn't care much for history.

"Yes," she said casually, sitting down in a big cushy

chair and crossing her long, slim legs. "History. As it happens, history has smiled upon Belle Gumph recently, and we feel you might want to reconsider your plans for her buildings."

"Aw, no." John turned to the window, as if calmly perusing the view, though he was anything but calm and he hardly noticed the view. Plainly and simply, he wasn't going to deal with the issue any further—he couldn't, he was afraid he'd start crying.

Peter, meanwhile, fell into the chair opposite her and folded his arms across his chest. "Get to the punch line, Katherine," he said.

"It's sort of a long story," she warned them, enjoying her moment.

"By definition, history is a long story," he said with a cloying grimace. In truth he was having a moment of his own, but it wouldn't do to let her see it. Just yet.

"Yes, of course. That's true, isn't it? Well . . . this story starts in the mid–seventeen hundreds, when the land we are presently discussing was deeded to one Herbert S. Albertson, a Belgian immigrant who wanted to be a farmer. He left his entire estate, including the land, to his son, Herbert S. Albertson, Jr., in 1801. The son apparently was a very prosperous farmer, as was *his* son, David Daniel Albertson, and *his* son, Herbert D. Albertson. Are you following me so far?" she asked politely, not wanting to leave them in the dust, so to speak. Peter gave one slow nod, and she continued, "Well, *his* son, Herbert D.'s, whose name was Joshua H. Albertson, took a different path in life. When the land came to him, he was forced to sell it to pay off some debts he'd gathered—as a result of a rather decadent lifestyle, I understand."

Peter yawned, blatantly.

"I can see you're on the edge of your seat there, so I'll get to the point."

"In this century, I hope."

"Joshua sold the land in parcels, starting with the fields furthest from the river, because, you see, he was very fond of the river and the house, the family estate house for a century and a half, was located there on the banks."

"Sooo . . . ?" he prompted her when she paused.

"Sooo . . . Joshua was not only a poor businessman, a scoundrel, and a terrible wretch, he was also a poet. Of course, in his time, well, actually, even in our time, he isn't considered to be much of a poet. But he did manage to get his work bound and published. And over the years he has gathered some notoriety—in that he is considered to be an excellent example of bad American literature."

She stopped to see if one or both of the brothers were getting a clear picture of the situation yet. John had turned from the window, and they were both staring at her, so she assumed they weren't and continued on.

"Of course, eventually Joshua was forced to sell his entire estate. The family home was torn down. The river prospered in trade shipping, which eventually took over the entire riverfront. Housing for dock workers was erected and—"

"No!" John shouted from across the room. "Don't say it. Don't you dare say it."

"Okay." She folded her hands in her lap and lowered her eyes. When she peeked up at them through a fringe of dark hair, her eyes were shining triumphantly.

Peter could hardly resist her. There was something about the spark in her eyes that he knew he'd never tire of.

"Go ahead. Get it over with," he said, the epitome of a defeated entrepreneur. "Say it."

"Well," she said, trying to appear to be the reluctant bearer of bad news. "As it turns out, two of the walls in one of Belle's buildings were originally foundations for the old Albertson manor house, and with Joshua being a poet of some note, Belle and I were thinking—"

"Okay. That's plenty," he said on second thought. "It might be better if you don't say it out loud. You even whisper Historical Society around a construction site and you may as well lay the whole damned crew off for the next two years at least."

"Yes, well, Belle and I had heard that somewhere. That's why we decided to come to you first. I mean, it is your construction site, and we thought perhaps you'd be willing to advise us as to what to do with all this interesting information."

"I'll tell you what to do with your interesting information," John muttered, beside himself. "This is blackmail."

"Certainly not." She looked aghast. "I'm an attorney, an officer of the court."

John made a rather snippy reference to the excrement of an adult male bovine animal, and Katherine smiled, understanding his point perfectly.

"Your information involves only one of the buildings," Peter said, sticking to the matter at hand.

"But my dear, sweet old client loves both her buildings," she said, batting her eyes at him. "She couldn't save one from destruction and not the other, now could she?"

"You can't get away with this," John said, pacing now. "The guy's a nothing, a nobody. A couple of rotten poems and— This isn't going to work, Katherine. That guy isn't even a half-line footnote in history. He won't save those buildings for you."

"True," she said, looking sad. "In the long run he probably won't. But the thing is," she held up her finger, "how long *is* the long run? Why, just a simple investigation by the Historical Society could take months, years, maybe. Of course, if you have some other project you can be working on during that time, it might not matter. But if you don't . . ."

"Are you going to let her get away with this?" John turned on Peter.

"I think she already has gotten away with it," he said, his blood pumping hard and fast and hot as he watched the lights in her eyes. "Short of hiring a couple of hit men to keep her and the old lady quiet, there doesn't seem to be much we can do to stop her. There's probably a letter somewhere, anyway."

He winked at her.

For the first time since she'd entered the room, Peter was dealing with her on a personal level. The wink was collusional, as if he'd known her plan all along, as if he'd been waiting for her to make the first move.

The emotions she'd set aside in the beginning, so as not to interfere with the business end of her visit, were back. They swung from star to star in the excitement of her love and her newfound discoveries, then plummeted to the earth with remorse and sorrow. They soared again with hope, and fell once more with hurt and anger.

"Come over here and look at this," John said, standing near a to-scale model design of the project. "Have you seen what you want to ruin? There's no place in this design for those two buildings."

Katherine let loose a sigh as she stood. She didn't mind blackmailing people. Sometimes it was as necessary an evil as plea bargaining or diminished sentences for testimony. It was an unspoken part of her job. What she did mind was tampering with someone else's work. In this case, work that was not only honest and aboveboard, but creative, artistic, and painstaking as well. This wasn't just bricks and concrete for the Wesley brothers, it was something they'd created from a dream, from their hearts.

Her worst enemy and oldest companion imposed itself on her conscience as she examined for the first time the Wesley brothers' design for the Safran River Vista Project. There were no words to describe it short of brilliant, innovative, and spectacular.

If not for the familiar bend in the river and the placement of several prominent preexisting landmarks, she wouldn't have recognized the area. It could have been any one of a number of elaborate boardwalks along the Atlantic coast. But it wasn't. It was the Safran River, old but always new; busy but slow flowing; heart of the city, too long ignored.

Sagging warehouses and dilapidated buildings were now sleek, unobtrusive shops, offices, and restaurants featuring floating decks, garden patios, and catwalks with magnificent views of the river. The street was tree-lined, with broad sidewalks and benches, and a good-sized park held a gazebo for summer music concerts. It was a mix of all that was new and amazing and all that was old, sweet, and wonderful.

"Oh, this is fabulous," she murmured in awe, her eyes skimming over the board again and again, taking in the details and the possibilities. "It's charming. Perfect."

"And finished," John said. "There's no room here for those two buildings."

"I can see that," she said, "but only because they aren't here. I mean, if they were as immoveable as the bend in the river, wouldn't you have built this around them, the way you did the bend?"

"Do you have any idea how long it took us to create this? To please everyone *and* keep it inside the budget? And now you want us to plop a couple of old, rat-infested buildings down in the middle of it and start all over?" John was looking at her as if she were some sort of fool.

"They aren't rat infested."

"Tell it to the EPA guys."

"I will," she said, then, looking down at the model, she said, "Surely you wouldn't have to start over from the beginning. Couldn't you incorporate them into this plan somehow?"

"They'd stick out like a couple of sore thumbs, ruin the skyline, the symmetry," he said, his patience tissue thin as he tried in vain to explain it once again.

"Maybe not," Peter said, looking smug.

"What do you mean, maybe not?" John blustered, and turned red in the face under the strain of this final straw—his brother's defection to the enemy. "Listen, what you do with this woman on your own time is up to you, but if you bring it into this office, then it becomes my business, too, and I won't stand for it. Don't even think of changing boats in the middle of this stream or I'll . . ."

"You'll what?" Peter asked simply, meeting his brother's gaze straight-on.

For a moment it looked as if the Wesleys were going to mix it up right there on the office floor. And for that moment, Katherine felt as if she'd gone too far once again. Driving a wedge between twins had never been her intent. If she caused a rift between them . . .

Inwardly she closed and bolted the door against her guilt and reminded herself that she was there to state facts and suggest alternatives. Whether or not the brothers came to blows was up to them. It had nothing to do with her. She wasn't responsible for their decisions or their behavior.

This new way of thinking was difficult for her. She had to repeat the concept over and over to keep from stepping between them.

However, it seemed that John's loud and mighty squall of anger couldn't withstand the calm, quiet strength of Peter's challenge. His confidence and the stamina of his character were not as well developed. He lowered his eyes in defeat and fought to control his ire.

Not a man to belabor a point well made, Peter stepped over to his desk and bent to remove a shoe box from a lower drawer. He returned to the model, looking pensive.

"This doesn't have to be the answer," he told them, remarkably humble and reticent for a man who just won a major battle with a single stare. "It's just a thought. An idea I had."

From the shoe box he removed an additional piece of the model and snapped it on the existing archetype. Connected to one another by an enclosed crosswalk and to the street below by gracefully curved stairwells on either side, were the top five floors of both of

Belle's buildings. They definitely stood out, but Peter had redesigned the exteriors to complement the rest of the project, and now they were like a huge H with its crossbar a long, comely ribbon trailing all the way to the ground on both sides.

Taken aback, John and Katherine stared at the layout. John was seeing it through an artist's eyes and was contemplative and discerning. Katherine, awed and fascinated, was seeing it through the eyes of a lover.

"When did you do this?" she asked, her throat tight with emotion.

"A few months ago." A vague shrug. "After the lunch. After I found out who you were."

"Why? Why did you do this?"

He could have told her that he did it because he loved her. He could have said that he did it for Belle or to impress her with his broad-mindedness or that he'd seen an injustice and acted upon it, or he did it because he'd been afraid of losing her. He could have answered that he did it to win her back. Instead, he told her the truth.

"I was afraid you weren't going to lose. I thought you'd win the appeal and we'd be set back another year and a half redesigning the project. It was a precaution."

There were no words to describe what Katherine was feeling, but it was easy to see it in her eyes. She had been unaware that in his loving, Peter had gone deeper and further into the discovery of who she was than anyone else had before. He had distinguished and set her apart from her sisters, from every other woman in the world, for that matter. He'd respected her for who she was and what she could do. He'd believed in her.

Their gazes met across the table. They didn't need words to say how much they'd missed each other. They didn't need to verbalize the regret they felt for spent words and for having hurt each other. They didn't need to speak aloud of the yearning in their hearts.

Still, it was as equally plain to them both that it was going to take more than a little cardboard and glue to mend the breach between them.

"Where are the structural prints for this?" John asked, oblivious to the true significance of his brother's creation and taking for granted his usual exacting thoroughness. "If we can get the engineers to okay them and the inspectors to take a look at them before we take them to the planning committee, we won't lose much time on this at all. In fact . . ."

The hows and wherefores were unimportant to Katherine. She'd done what she'd come to do, and while the brothers jumped into the renovations like a couple of kids with a new rubber swimming pool, Katherine slipped out of the office.

Retracing her steps to the elevators, she lost a lot of the self-contentment she'd had when she'd first arrived. Satisfaction in a job well done wasn't enough to fill the wide gaps of sadness and regret she felt in not being able to share her victory with Peter.

It was too much to ask for, even for her, to best

him and then hope that all would be right between them again. Tears blurred her vision as her mind filled with what-might-have-beens. She wished she'd known how much he'd believed in her; it might have been different for them. She wished he'd told her about his precautionary redesigning; it might have been different for them. She wished she'd believed in him more and doubted herself less; it might have been . . .

"Hey!" Peter called, rushing through the glass doors to beat the elevators. He was surprised and confused to find her leaving. "Where are you going?"

Her spirit did another high-low swing between hope and dejection—and got stuck in discouragement.

"Home," she said. And to bed, she thought, the drain of the past several weeks suddenly catching up to her. "I'm tired."

He laughed. "I bet you're the only lawyer in the world who gets depressed when you win."

"I didn't win. Not the way I wanted to win, anyway."

"Is that why you're depressed?"

"I'm not depressed."

"You're not? Your eyes look sad."

"My eyes are exhausted. Belle kept me up all night long, dodging falling boxes and reading me terrible poetry."

"No," he said, scrutinizing her face too carefully for her peace of mind. "I know those eyes. They talk to me. And they're more than just sleepy."

"Will you stay out of my eyes?" she asked, unreasonably annoyed. "I mean, leave my eyes alone. They don't talk. I talk. If you want to know how I feel about something, ask me, don't ask my eyes. I mean, don't imagine that you can read things in them and presume to know what I'm thinking and how I feel."

She ought to talk to herself in a mirror sometime, he thought, watching her struggle with her emotions. If eyes could talk, hers would be hoarse from wailing in pain and turmoil, and whimpering with need and unhappiness.

"So? What are you thinking? How do you feel?"

"I'm thinking this is a very slow elevator."

"What about us?"

"What about us?" she asked, muscles tensing, her stomach rolling and vibrating as if she'd had Mexican jumping beans for breakfast.

"What do you think about us? How do you feel about me?"

"I think . . ." she hesitated. She looked back toward the offices, then at Peter. "I think what you did back there was pretty terrific. Thank you."

He frowned. "That's it? That's all you're thinking?"

She chewed the inside of her lip thoughtfully. He wasn't telling much about his thoughts or feelings. His expression was intense but guarded. She sensed that he was reaching out to her, but she couldn't tell if it was with both arms to embrace her and hold her tight or simply an extended hand to end what they had in a cordial fashion.

"No, I'm thinking also that I'd like to thank you for being honest with me. I've learned a lot about myself in the past few months. Things that I might not have ever known if I hadn't met you. And, well, I don't feel as if it's been a total loss. You and me, I mean. I'm not sorry. For any of it."

His frown deepened. A spark of panic flashed in his eyes.

"You're not thinking it's over, are you?"

"Isn't it?" Her brows rose in surprise and confusion.

"Hell, no. We've got at least fifty years on earth and the rest of eternity to fill before it's over. We've just started."

"You don't hate me?" she asked, scowling. Feelings that had been cut off for weeks came suddenly awake. And much as when a body part falls asleep from disuse, they came back prickling with pain and anger. "You don't think I'm self-centered and irreparably screwed up with guilt and an overactive sense of responsibility? You don't think I live in a fantasyland? I'm not an idealist with a weak character who either has to have a scapegoat for everything that goes wrong or offer myself as a martyr to the cause?"

"No."

"Liar." The word was as good as a slap on the face. "I'm all those things. Everything you said about me was true."

He opened his mouth to deny it, to retract his words, but the fury in her eyes stopped him.

"I don't hate you," he said, picking the only argument he had a chance of winning. "I'm crazy in love with you, and I don't really care about all that other stuff." He paused. "I do care, but only because I think you always serve yourself last, give yourself the smallest piece of the cake, take your own happiness after you've made sure that everyone has theirs. It's all part of what I love about you, but you deserve better."

"Damn straight, I deserve better," she said, stepping sideways to punch the elevator button impatiently. "And from now on that's what I'm taking. Only the best."

He got the distinct impression that she didn't consider him to be the best of anything. He'd hurt her too deeply. She was leaving him. And if he let her go, he'd never see her again.

"Katherine," he said, then became aware of several office workers approaching the elevators. "Katherine. Can we talk? Will you let me explain?"

She turned and held her hand out to him. He took it gladly. She shook it, coolly, professionally.

"There's nothing to explain. You told me the truth, and I'm grateful." He wouldn't let go of her hand. Then again, if he had let go, she'd have kicked him. She was angry . . . and so happy and so much in love she could hardly think straight. "What you did today was terrific. Belle will be a happy old woman."

"I want to make you a happy old woman," he said. Heads turned in their direction, and he felt a flush of heat rise up his neck. "Katherine. We need to talk. Come back inside."

He tried to pull her back toward the office, but she wouldn't budge. She was imagining the topic of conversation in the ladies' room for the next few days and smiled in her heart. Maybe it was time for some serious groveling.

"No. I don't think so," she said. "I think we've said all we need to say to each other."

"But, Katherine, we—"

"No. Don't you think we've hurt each other enough?"

"Yes, I do. I think it's time we—"

"Said good-bye? I agree. Good-bye, Peter."

Peter's eyes narrowed dangerously.

"Fine," he said, turning on his heel to leave her.

Was that it? Was that all the groveling he was going to do?

An elevator arrived, and their audience walked reluctantly inside, anxious to see if she'd follow them. Their leaving was a minor disappointment to Katherine, because she wasn't finished with Peter Wesley.

"There is one last thing that needs to be said," she decided, rounding on him as the doors closed on act one and act two began. He turned slowly to face her, his anger unconcealed. She was feeling giddy and reckless and flaunted herself in the face of danger. "I don't like being accused of doing something I haven't even thought about doing yet."

His gaze shifted, searching for the meaning of her words.

"Who are you to assume that you know what I'm going to think or do before *I* know what I'm going to think or do?" she asked. "I never said that I thought you'd manipulated me professionally. I never thought it until that day on the boat, and then I rejected the idea as quickly as it came to me. And if you had to beg me to believe that the way you harassed Belle and her tenants wasn't rotten and underhanded, it's because it was rotten and underhanded. Standard play doesn't make it right. And making those old people walk two blocks to the bus stop before it was necessary just stinks."

"You're right," he said after a moment's consideration.

"I know," she said, indignant.

"Is there anything else?"

"Yes. There is," she said, taking two steps toward him. "When *I* decide to choose my career over the man I love, I'll let you know. I don't want you running around second-guessing me all the time. You know me pretty well, but you don't know everything."

A smile tugged at his lips as hope bloomed in his heart.

Another one of the many things he loved about Katherine Asher was that you didn't have to hit her on the head with a blunt object more than once to focus her attention on a specific problem and that, as a problem solver by nature, she would attack and correct it with a vengeance. Had he really thought she needed to learn to stand up for herself?

"I don't know anything really," she said quietly. "Except that I was scared and I took it out on you."

"Scared? Of what?" she asked, looking at him.

"Losing you. I was afraid that those buildings would come between us, so I set up a detour, like a fireline, you know? Like when they destroy a ring of trees around a forest fire to keep it from spreading?"

"So you hurt me to keep me from destroying our relationship?" she asked, her insides turning sour with anger and resentment.

"That's how it sounds, doesn't it?" he said, hearing it the way she did and hating it. "But I didn't mean for it to be like that. I didn't enjoy hurting you. I know . . ."

The elevator returned. Two men in suits stepped out and walked down the hall.

Katherine and Peter looked at each other, questioning. She had an escape route. Should she leave or listen? Would she get in? Could he stop her?

Taking no chances, he stepped in and pushed every button from the sixteenth floor to the parking garage. Stepping out, he took her by the shoulders and held her till the doors closed.

"Katherine, I know I hurt you and I'm sorry. More than you'll ever know," he said. "Looking back on it, I know I handled it all wrong, but I didn't know what else to do. I was angry and scared. I went away so we'd both be frightened, and I was mean so we'd both be mad. Then I attacked the most vulnerable target I could find to distract you. Your conscience. I knew you'd feel guilty if you lost the hearing. And I knew you'd feel guilty if you thought you'd destroyed what we had together. What I'd hoped you'd do was make a choice. I tried to force you to make a choice you couldn't make. Between being who you are . . . and me."

He let loose a small ironic chuckle as he cupped her cheek in his hand. "It was a no-win choice. I couldn't love you any way but the way you are."

"The way I *was*? Or the way I am now?"

"Any way you want. Anyone you want to be. By any other name. I'll always love you the same."

She gave him a dubious look.

"That's big talk for someone who's not a lawyer," she said.

He grinned.

"I thought big talk was all they understood."

"Some of them understand truth and sincerity too."

"Well, what would I have to do to persuade you that I'm true and sincere?" he asked, his hands sliding down her arms to her waist as he recognized the not-so-subtle light in her eyes.

"Let's see now," she pondered, stepping into his loose embrace. "Can you run faster than a speeding bullet?"

"Sure. But then I'd be too tired to do anything else."

"Oh. Well then, how about swimming the ocean?"

"That'd take too long."

"Can you lasso a star?"

"Ecologically unsound."

"Sit on a flagpole?"

He cringed. "Too painful."

"How about alligator wrestling?"

"I thought you thought that was stupid?"

"Oh, yeah." She touched his face. In it she saw his remorse, his love, his hope. He had a beautiful face. He was a handsome man with nearly as many flaws as she had. He made mistakes too. He was terribly human, just like her. And she loved him with all that she was. "I guess that leaves jumping tall buildings, huh?"

He looked deep into her eyes and found his forgiveness, his life, his future.

He nodded slowly and grinned. "I could do that, jump a tall building. But if it's all the same to you, I'd much rather jump something else. . . ."

THE EDITOR'S CORNER

Summer is here at last, and we invite you to join us for our 11th anniversary. Things are really heating up with six wonderful new Loveswepts that sizzle with sexy heroes and dazzling heroines. As always, our romances are packed with tender emotion and steamy passion that are guaranteed to make this summer a hot one!

Always a favorite, Helen Mittermeyer gives us a heroine who is **MAGIC IN PASTEL**, Loveswept #690. When fashion model Pastel Marx gazes at Will Nordstrom, it's as if an earthquake hits him! Will desires her with an intensity that shocks him, but the anguish she tries to hide makes him want to protect her. Determined to help Pastel fight the demons that plague her, Will tries to comfort her, longing to know why his fairy-tale princess is imprisoned by her fear. Enveloped in the arms of a man whose touch soothes and arouses, Pastel struggles to accept the gift of his caring and keep their rare love true in a world of fire and ice. Helen delivers a story with characters that will warm your heart.

The heroine in Deborah Harmse's newest book finds herself **IN THE ARMS OF THE LAW,** Loveswept #691. Rebekah de Bieren decides Detective Mackenzie Hoyle has a handsome face, a great body, and a rotten attitude! When Mack asks Becky to help him persuade one of her students to testify in a murder case, he is stunned by this pint-sized blond angel who is as tempting as she is tough . . . but he refuses to take no for an answer—no matter how her blue eyes flash. Becky hears the sorrow behind Mack's cynical request and senses the tormented emotions he hides beneath his fierce dedication. Drawn to the fire she sees sparking in his cool gray eyes, she responds with shameless abandon—and makes him yearn for impossible dreams. Deborah Harmse will have you laughing and crying with this sexy romance.

FOR MEN ONLY, Loveswept #692, by the wonderfully talented Sally Goldenbaum, is a romance that cooks. The first time Ellie Livingston and Pete Webster met, he'd been a blind date from hell, but now he looks good enough to eat! Pete definitely has his doubts about taking a cooking class she's designed just for men, but his gaze is hungry for the pleasures only she can provide. Pete has learned not to trust beautiful women, but Ellie's smile is real—and full of temptation. Charmed by her spicy personality and passionate honesty, he revels in the sensual magic she weaves, but can Pete make her believe their love is enough? **FOR MEN ONLY** is a story you can really sink your teeth into.

Glenna McReynolds has given us another dark and dangerous hero in **THE DRAGON AND THE DOVE,** Loveswept #693. Cooper Daniels had asked for a female shark with an instinct for the jugular, but instead he's sent an angelfish in silk who looks too innocent to help him with his desperate quest to avenge his brother's death! Jessica Langston is fascinated by the hard sensuality of his face and mesmerized by eyes that meet hers with the force of a head-on collisic ,, but she refuses to be dismissed—winning Cooper's respect and igniting his desire. Suddenly, Cooper is compelled by an inexorable need to claim her with tantalizing gentleness. Her surrender makes him yearn to rediscover the tenderness he's missed, but Cooper believes he'll only hurt the woman who has given him back his life. Jessica cherishes her tough hero, but now she must help heal the wounds that haunt his soul. **THE DRAGON AND THE DOVE** is Glenna at her heart-stopping best.

Donna Kauffman invites you to **TANGO IN PARADISE**, Loveswept #694. Jack Tango is devastatingly virile, outrageously seductive, and a definite danger to her peace of mind, but resort owner April Morgan needs his help enough to promise him whatever he wants—and she suspects what he wants is her in his arms! Jack wants her desperately but without regrets—and he'll wait until she pleads for his touch. April responds with wanton satisfaction to Jack's need to claim her soul, to possess and pleasure her, but even with him as her formidable ally, does she dare face old ghosts? **TANGO IN PARADISE** will show you why Donna is one of our brightest and fastest-rising stars.

Last, but definitely not least, is a battle of passion and will in Linda Wisdom's **O'HARA vs. WILDER**, Loveswept #695. For five years, Jake Wilder had been the man of her sexiest dreams, the best friend and partner she'd once dared to love, then leave, but seeing him again in the flesh leaves Tess O'Hara breathless . . . and wildly aroused! Capturing her mouth in a kiss that sears her to the toes and catches him in the fire-storm, Jake knows she is still more woman than any man can handle, but he is willing to try. Powerless to resist the kisses that brand her his forever, Tess fights the painful memories that their reckless past left her, but Jake insists they are a perfect team, in bed and out. Seduced by the electricity sizzling between them, tantalized beyond reason by Jake's wicked grin and rough edges, Tess wonders if a man who's always looked for trouble can settle for all she can give him. Linda Wisdom has another winner with **O'HARA vs. WILDER.**

Happy reading,

With warmest wishes,

Nita Taublib

Nita Taublib
Associate Publisher

P.S. Don't miss the women's novels coming your way in June—**WHERE SHADOWS GO,** by Eugenia Price, is an enthralling love story of the Old South that is the second volume of the *Georgia Trilogy,* following **BRIGHT CAPTIVITY; DARK JOURNEY,** by award-winning Sandra Canfield, is a heart-wrenching story of love and obsession, betrayal and forgiveness, in which a woman discovers the true price of forbidden passion; **SOMETHING BORROWED, SOMETHING BLUE,** by Jillian Karr, is a mixture of romance and suspense in which four brides—each with a dangerous secret—will be the focus of a deliciously glamorous issue of *Perfect Bride* magazine; and finally **THE MOON RIDER,** Virginia Lynn's most appealing historical romance to date, is a passionate tale of a highwayman and his lady-love. We'll be giving you a sneak peek at these wonderful books in next month's LOVESWEPTs. And immediately following this page look for a preview of the terrific romances from Bantam that are *available now!*

Don't miss these fantastic books by your favorite Bantam authors

On sale in April:

DECEPTION
by Amanda Quick

RELENTLESS
by Patricia Potter

SEIZED BY LOVE
by Susan Johnson

WILD CHILD
by Suzanne Forster

THE NEW YORK TIMES BESTSELLING NOVEL

DECEPTION
by *Amanda Quick*

"One of the hottest and most prolific writers in romance today . . . Her heroines are always spunky women you'd love to know and her heroes are dashing guys you'd love to love."
—USA Today

NOW AVAILABLE IN PAPERBACK WHEREVER BANTAM BOOKS ARE SOLD

Patricia Potter

Nationally Bestselling Author
Of **Notorious** and **Renegade**

RELENTLESS

*Beneath the outlaw's smoldering gaze, Shea Randall felt
a stab of pure panic . . . and a shiver of shocking desire.
Held against her will by the darkly handsome bandit,
she knew that for her father's sake she must find a
way to escape. Only later, as the days of her captivity
turned into weeks and Rafe Tyler's fiery passion sparked
her own, did Shea fully realize her perilous position—
locked in a mountain lair with a man who could steal
her heart . . .*

The door opened, and the bright light of the
afternoon sun almost blinded her. Her eyes were
drawn to the large figure in the doorway. Silhou-
etted by the sun behind him, Tyler seemed even
bigger, stronger, more menacing. She had to force
herself to keep from backing away.

He hesitated, his gaze raking over the cabin,
raking over her. He frowned at the candle.

She stood. It took all her bravery, but she stood,
forcing her eyes to meet his, to determine what was
there. There seemed to be nothing but a certain
coolness.

"I'm thirsty," she said. It came out as more of a challenge than a request, and she saw a quick flicker of something in his eyes. She hoped it was remorse, but that thought was quickly extinguished by his reply.

"Used to better places?" It was a sneer, plain and simple, and Shea felt anger stirring again.

"I'm used to gentlemen and simple . . . humanity."

"That's strange, considering your claim that you're Randall's daughter."

"I haven't claimed anything to you."

"That's right, you haven't," he agreed in a disagreeable voice. "You haven't said much at all."

"And I don't intend to. Not to a thief and a traitor."

"Be careful, Miss Randall. Your . . . continued health depends on this thief and traitor."

"That's supposed to comfort me?" Her tone was pure acid.

His gaze stabbed her. "You'll have to forgive me. I'm out of practice in trying to comfort anyone. Ten years out of practice."

"So you're going to starve me?"

"No," he said slowly. "I'm not going to do *that*."

The statement was ominous to Shea. "What are you going to do?"

"Follow my rules, and I won't do anything."

"You already are. You're keeping me here against my will."

He was silent for a moment, and Shea noted a muscle moving in his neck, as if he were just barely restraining himself.

"Lady, because of your . . . father, I was 'held'

against my will for ten years." She wanted to slap him for his mockery. She wanted to kick him where it would hurt the most. But now was not the time.

"Is that it? You're taking revenge out on me?"

The muscle in his cheek moved again. "No, Miss Randall, it's not that. You just happened to be in the wrong place at the wrong time. I don't have any more choices than you do." He didn't know why in the hell he was explaining, except her last charge galled him.

"You do."

He turned away from her. "Believe what you want," he said, his voice indifferent. "Blow out that candle and come with me if you want some water."

She didn't want to go with him, but she was desperate to shake her thirst. She blew out the candle, hoping that once outside he wouldn't see dried streaks of tears on her face. She didn't want to give him that satisfaction.

She didn't have to worry. He paid no attention to her, and she had to scurry to keep up with his long-legged strides. She knew she was plain, especially so in the loose-fitting britches and shirt she wore and with her hair in a braid. She also knew she should be grateful that he was indifferent to her, but a part of her wanted to goad him, confuse him . . . attract him.

Shea felt color flood her face. To restrain her train of thought, she concentrated on her surroundings.

Her horse was gone, although her belongings were propped against the tree stump. There was a shack to the left, and she noticed a lock on the door. That must be where he'd taken the weapons and where he kept his own horse. The keys must be in his pockets. He strode over to the building and picked up a bucket with his gloved hand.

She tried to pay attention to their route, but it seemed they had just melted into the woods and everything looked alike. She thought of turning around and running, but he was only a couple of feet ahead of her.

He stopped abruptly at a stream and leaned against a tree, watching her.

She had never drunk from a stream before, yet that was obviously what he expected her to do. The dryness in her mouth was worse, and she couldn't wait. She moved to the edge of the stream and kneeled, feeling awkward and self-conscious, knowing he was watching and judging. She scooped up a handful of water, then another, trying to sip it before it leaked through her fingers. She caught just enough to be tantalized.

She finally fell flat on her stomach and put her mouth in the water, taking long swallows of the icy cold water, mindless of the way the front of her shirt got soaked, mindless of anything but water.

It felt wonderful and tasted wonderful. When she was finally sated, she reluctantly sat up, and her gaze went to Tyler.

His stance was lazy but his eyes, like fine emeralds, were intense with fire. She felt a corresponding wave of heat consume her. She couldn't move her gaze from him, no matter how hard she tried. It was as if they were locked together.

He was the first to divert his gaze and his face settled quickly into its usual indifferent mask.

She looked down and noticed that her wet shirt clung to her, outlining her breasts. She swallowed hard and turned around. She splashed water on her face, hoping it would cool the heat suffusing her body.

She kept expecting Tyler to order her away, but he didn't. And she lingered as long as she could. She didn't want to go back to the dark cabin. She didn't want to face him, or those intense emotions she didn't understand.

She felt his gaze on her, and knew she should feel fear. He had been in prison a very long time. But she was certain he wouldn't touch her in a sexual way.

Because he despises you.

Because he despises your father.

She closed her eyes for a moment, and when she opened them, a spiral of light gleamed through the trees, hitting the stream. She wanted to reach out and catch that sunbeam, to climb it to some safe place.

But there were no safe places any longer.

She watched that ray of light until it slowly dissipated as the sun slipped lower in the sky, and then she turned around again. She hadn't expected such patience from Tyler.

"Ready?" he asked in his hoarse whisper.

The word held many meanings.

Ready for what? She wasn't ready for any of this.

But she nodded.

He sauntered over and offered his hand.

She refused it and rose by herself, stunned by how much she suddenly wanted to take his hand, to feel that strength again.

And Shea realized her battle wasn't entirely with him. It was also with herself.

"Susan Johnson brings sensuality to new heights and beyond."
—*Romantic Times*

SUSAN JOHNSON
Nationally bestselling author of **Outlaw** and **Silver Flame**

SEIZED BY LOVE
Now available in paperback

Sweeping from the fabulous country estates and hunting lodges to the opulent ballrooms and salons of the Russian nobility, here is a novel of savage passions and dangerous pleasures by the incomparable Susan Johnson, mistress of the erotic historical.

"*Under your protection?*" Alisa sputtered, flushing vividly as the obvious and unmistakable clarity of his explanation struck her. Of course, she should have realized. How very stupid of her. The full implication of what the public reaction to her situation would be left her momentarily stunned, devoured with shame. She was exceedingly thankful, for the first time since her parents' death, that they *weren't* alive to see the terrible depths to which she had fallen, the sordid fate outlined for her.

Irritated at the masterful certainty of Nikki's assumption, and resentful to be treated once more like a piece of property, she coldly said, "I don't recall placing myself under your protection."

"Come now, love," Nikki said reasonably, "if you recall, when I found you in that shed, your alternatives were surely limited; more severe beatings and possibly death if Forseus had continued drugging you. Hardly a choice of options, I should think. And consider it now," Nikki urged amiably, "plenty of advantages, especially if one has already shown a *decided* partiality for the man one has as protector. I'm not considered ungenerous, and if you contrive to please me in the future as well as you have to this date, we shall deal together quite easily."

Taking umbrage at his arrogant presumption that her role was to please *him*, Alisa indignantly said, "I haven't any *decided* partiality for you, you arrogant lecher, and furthermore—"

"Give me three minutes alone with you, my dear," Nikki interjected suavely, "and I feel sure I can restore my credit on that account."

Her eyes dropped shamefully before his candid regard, but she was angry enough to thrust aside the brief feeling of embarrassment, continuing belligerently. "Maria has some money of mine she brought with us. I'm not in *need* of protection."

"Not enough to buy you one decent gown, let alone support yourself, a child, and three servants," Nikki disagreed bluntly with his typical disregard for tact.

"Well, then," Alisa insisted heatedly, "I'm relatively well educated, young, and strong. I can obtain a position as governess."

"I agree in principle with your idea, but unfortunately, the pressures of existence in this world of travail serve to daunt the most optimistic hopes." His words were uttered in a lazy, mocking drawl. "For you, the role of governess"—the sarcasm in his voice was all too apparent—"is quite a pleasant conceit, my dear. You *will* forgive my speaking frankly, but I fear you are lacking in a sense of the realities of things.

"*If*—I say, *if*—any wife in her right mind would allow a provokingly beautiful young woman like yourself to enter her household, I'd wager a small fortune, the master of that house would be sharing your bed within the week. Consider the folly of the notion, love. At least with me there'd be no indignant wife to throw you and your retinue out into the street when her husband's preferences became obvious. And since I have a rather intimate knowledge of many of these wives, I think my opinion is to be relied upon. And as your protector," he continued equably, "I, of course, feel an obligation to maintain your daughter and servants in luxurious comfort."

"I am not a plaything to be bought!" Alisa said feelingly.

"Ah, my dear, but you are. Confess, it is a woman's role, primarily a pretty plaything for a man's pleasure and then inexorably as night follows day—a mother. Those are the two roles a woman plays. It's preordained. Don't fight it," he said practically.

Alisa would have done anything, she felt at that moment, to wipe that detestable look of smugness from Nikki's face.

"Perhaps I'll take Cernov up on his offer after all," she said with the obvious intent to provoke. "Is he richer than you? I must weigh the advantages if

I'm to make my way profitably in the demimonde," she went on calculatingly. "Since I'm merely a plaything, it behooves me to turn a practical frame of mind to the role of demirep and sell myself for the highest price in money and rank obtainable. I have a certain refinement of background—"

"Desist in the cataloguing if you please," he broke in rudely, and in a dangerously cold voice murmured, "Let us not cavil over trifles. You're staying with me." Alisa involuntarily quailed before the stark, open challenge in his eyes, and her heart sank in a most unpleasant way.

"So my life is a trifle?" she whispered, trembling with a quiet inner violence.

"You misunderstand, my dear," the even voice explained with just a touch of impatience. "It's simply that I don't intend to enter into any senseless wrangles or debates over your attributes and the direction in which your favors are to be bestowed. Madame, you're to remain my mistress." His lips smiled faintly but the smile never reached his eyes.

WILD CHILD
by Suzanne Forster
bestselling author of
SHAMELESS

"A storyteller of incandescent brilliance . . . beyond compare in a class by herself . . . that rare
talent, a powerhouse writer whose extraordinary sensual touch can mesmerize . . ."
—*Romantic Times*

*Her memorable characters and sizzling tales of romance
and adventure have won her numerous awards and
countless devoted readers. Now, with her trademark
blend of intense sensuality and deep emotion, Suzanne
Forster reunites adversaries who share a tangled past—
and for whom an old spark of conflict will kindle into a
dangerously passionate blaze . . .*

"I want to talk about us," he said.

"Us?"

Blake could have predicted the stab of panic
in her eyes, but he couldn't have predicted what
was happening inside Cat. As she met his gaze,
she felt herself dropping, a wind-rider caught in
a powerful downdrift. The plummeting sensation
in her stomach was sudden and sharp. The dock
seemed to go out from under her feet, and as she
imagined herself falling, she caught a glimpse of
something in her mind that riveted her.

Surrender.

Even the glimpse of such naked emotion was
terrifying to Cat. It entranced and enthralled her. It

was the source of her panic. It was the wellspring of her deepest need. To be touched, to be loved. She shuddered in silence and raised her face to his.

By the time he did touch her, the shuddering was deep inside her. It was emotional and sexual and beautiful. No, she thought, this is impossible. This isn't happening. *Not with this man. Not with him . . .*

He curved his hand to her throat and drew her to him.

"What do I do, Cat?" he asked. "How do I make the sadness go away?"

The question rocked her softly, reverberating in the echo chamber her senses had become. *Not this man. Not him. He's hurt you too much. . . .*

"Sweet, sad, Cat." He caressed the underside of her chin with long, long strokes of his thumb. The sensations were soft and erotic and thrilling, and they accomplished exactly what they were supposed to, Cat realized, bringing her head up sharply. He wanted her to look up at him. He wanted her throat arched, her head tilted back.

No, Cat! He's hurt you too much.

"Don't," she whispered. "Not you . . ."

"Yes, Cat, me," he said. "It has to be me."

He bent toward her, and his lips touched hers with a lightning stroke of tenderness. Cat swallowed the moan in her throat. In all her guilty dreams of kissing Blake Wheeler—and there had been many—she had never imagined it as tender. She never had imagined a sweetness so sharp that it would fill her throat and tear through her heart like a poignant memory. Was this how lovers kissed? Lovers who had hurt each other and now needed to be very, very cautious? Lovers whose wounds weren't healed?

Age-old warnings stirred inside her. She should have resisted, she wanted to resist, but as his lips brushed over hers she felt yearnings flare up inside her—a wrenchingly sweet need to deepen the kiss, to be held and crushed in his arms. She had imagined him as self-absorbed, an egotistical lover who would take what he wanted and assume that being with him was enough for any woman. A night with Blake Wheeler. A night in heaven! She had imagined herself rejecting him, ordering him out of her bed and out of her life. She had imagined all of those things so many times . . . but never *tenderness*.

His mouth was warm. It was as vibrant as the water sparkling around them. She touched his arm, perhaps to push him away, and then his lips drifted over hers, and her touch became a caress. Her fingers shimmered over heat and muscle, and she felt a sudden, sharp need to be closer.

All of her attention was focused on the extraordinary thing that was happening to her. A kiss, she told herself, *it was just a kiss*. But he touched her with such rare tenderness. His fingers plucked at her nerve-strings as if she were a delicate musical instrument. His mouth transfused her with fire and drained her of energy at the same time. And when at last his arms came around her and brought her up against him, she felt a sweet burst of physical longing that saturated her senses.

She had dreamt of his body, too. And the feel of him now was almost more reality than she could stand. His thighs were steel, and his pelvic bones dug into her flesh. He was hard, righteously hard, and even the slightest shifts in pressure put her in touch with her own keening emptiness.

His tongue stroked her lips, and she opened

them to him slowly, irresistibly. On some level she knew she was playing a sword dance with her own emotions, tempting fate, tempting heartbreak, but the sensations were so exquisite, she couldn't stop herself. They seemed as inevitable and sensual as the deep currents swaying beneath them.

The first gliding touch of his tongue against hers electrified her. A gasp welled in her throat as he grazed her teeth and tingled sensitive surfaces. The penetration was deliciously languid and deep. By the time he lifted his mouth from hers, she was shocked and reeling from the taste of him.

The urge to push him away was instinctive.

"No, Cat," he said softly, inexplicably, "it's mine now. The sadness inside you is mine."

Studying her face, searching her eyes for something, he smoothed her hair and murmured melting suggestions that she couldn't consciously decipher. They tugged at her sweetly, hotly, pulling her insides to and fro, eliciting yearnings. Cat's first awareness of them was a kind of vague astonishment. It was deep and thrilling, what was happening inside her, like eddying water, like the sucking and pulling of currents. She'd never known such oddly captivating sensations.

The wooden dock creaked and the bay swelled gently beneath them, tugging at the pilings. Cat sighed as the rhythms of the sea and the man worked their enchantment. His hands *were* telepathic. They sought out all her tender spots. His fingers moved in concert with the deep currents, stroking the sideswells of her breasts, arousing her nerves to rivulets of excitement.

"Wild," he murmured as he cupped her breasts in his palms. "Wild, wild child."

And don't miss these spectacular
romances from Bantam Books,
on sale in May:

DARK JOURNEY
by the bestselling author
Sandra Canfield
"(Ms. Canfield's) superb style of writing
proves her to be an author extraordinaire."
—*Affaire de Coeur*

SOMETHING BORROWED SOMETHING BLUE
by
Jillian Karr
"Author Jillian Karr . . . explodes onto the
mainstream fiction scene . . . Great reading."
—*Romantic Times*

THE MOON RIDER
by the highly acclaimed
Virginia Lynn
"A master storyteller."
—*Rendezvous*

OFFICIAL RULES

To enter the sweepstakes below carefully follow all instructions found elsewhere in this offer.

The **Winners Classic** will award prizes with the following approximate maximum values: 1 Grand Prize: $26,500 (or $25,000 cash alternate); 1 First Prize: $3,000; 5 Second Prizes: $400 each; 35 Third Prizes: $100 each; 1,000 Fourth Prizes: $7.50 each. Total maximum retail value of Winners Classic Sweepstakes is $42,500. Some presentations of this sweepstakes may contain individual entry numbers corresponding to one or more of the aforementioned prize levels. To determine the Winners, individual entry numbers will first be compared with the winning numbers preselected by computer. For winning numbers not returned, prizes will be awarded in random drawings from among all eligible entries received. Prize choices may be offered at various levels. If a winner chooses an automobile prize, all license and registration fees, taxes, destination charges and, other expenses not offered herein are the responsibility of the winner. If a winner chooses a trip, travel must be complete within one year from the time the prize is awarded. Minors must be accompanied by an adult. Travel companion(s) must also sign release of liability. Trips are subject to space and departure availability. Certain black-out dates may apply.

The following applies to the sweepstakes named above:

No purchase necessary. You can also enter the sweepstakes by sending your name and address to: P.O. Box 508, Gibbstown, N.J. 08027. Mail each entry separately. Sweepstakes begins 6/1/93. Entries must be received by 12/30/94. Not responsible for lost, late, damaged, misdirected, illegible or postage due mail. Mechanically reproduced entries are not eligible. All entries become property of the sponsor and will not be returned.

Prize Selection/Validations: Selection of winners will be conducted no later than 5:00 PM on January 28, 1995, by an independent judging organization whose decisions are final. Random drawings will be held at 1211 Avenue of the Americas, New York, N.Y. 10036. Entrants need not be present to win. Odds of winning are determined by total number of entries received. Circulation of this sweepstakes is estimated not to exceed 200 million. All prizes are guaranteed to be awarded and delivered to winners. Winners will be notified by mail and may be required to complete an affidavit of eligibility and release of liability which must be returned within 14 days of date on notification or alternate winners will be selected in a random drawing. Any prize notification letter or any prize returned to a participating sponsor, Bantam Doubleday Dell Publishing Group, Inc., its participating divisions or subsidiaries, or the independent judging organization as undeliverable will be awarded to an alternate winner. Prizes are not transferable. No substitution for prizes except as offered or as may be necessary due to unavailability, in which case a prize of equal or greater value will be awarded. Prizes will be awarded approximately 90 days after the drawing. All taxes are the sole responsibility of the winners. Entry constitutes permission (except where prohibited by law) to use winners' names, hometowns, and likenesses for publicity purposes without further or other compensation. Prizes won by minors will be awarded in the name of parent or legal guardian.

Participation: Sweepstakes open to residents of the United States and Canada, except for the province of Quebec. Sweepstakes sponsored by Bantam Doubleday Dell Publishing Group, Inc., (BDD), 1540 Broadway, New York, NY 10036. Versions of this sweepstakes with different graphics and prize choices will be offered in conjunction with various solicitations or promotions by different subsidiaries and divisions of BDD. Where applicable, winners will have their choice of any prize offered at level won. Employees of BDD, its divisions, subsidiaries, advertising agencies, independent judging organization, and their immediate family members are not eligible.

Canadian residents, in order to win, must first correctly answer a time limited arithmetical skill testing question. Void in Puerto Rico, Quebec and wherever prohibited or restricted by law. Subject to all federal, state, local and provincial laws and regulations. For a list of major prize winners (available after 1/29/95): send a self-addressed, stamped envelope entirely separate from your entry to: Sweepstakes Winners, P.O. Box 517, Gibbstown, NJ 08027. Requests must be received by 12/30/94. DO NOT SEND ANY OTHER CORRESPONDENCE TO THIS P.O. BOX.

Bestselling Women's Fiction

Sandra Brown

_____	28951-9 TEXAS! LUCKY	$5.99/6.99 in Canada
_____	28990-X TEXAS! CHASE	$5.99/6.99
_____	29500-4 TEXAS! SAGE	$5.99/6.99
_____	29085-1 22 INDIGO PLACE	$5.99/6.99
_____	29783-X A WHOLE NEW LIGHT	$5.99/6.99
_____	56045-X TEMPERATURES RISING	$5.99/6.99
_____	56274-6 FANTA C	$4.99/5.99
_____	56278-9 LONG TIME COMING	$4.99/5.99

Amanda Quick

_____	28354-5 SEDUCTION	$5.99/6.99
_____	28932-2 SCANDAL	$5.99/6.99
_____	28594-7 SURRENDER	$5.99/6.99
_____	29325-7 RENDEZVOUS	$5.99/6.99
_____	29316-8 RECKLESS	$5.99/6.99
_____	29316-8 RAVISHED	$4.99/5.99
_____	29317-6 DANGEROUS	$5.99/6.99
_____	56506-0 DECEPTION	$5.99/7.50

Nora Roberts

_____	29078-9 GENUINE LIES	$5.99/6.99
_____	28578-5 PUBLIC SECRETS	$5.99/6.99
_____	26461-3 HOT ICE	$5.99/6.99
_____	26574-1 SACRED SINS	$5.99/6.99
_____	27859-2 SWEET REVENGE	$5.99/6.99
_____	27283-7 BRAZEN VIRTUE	$5.99/6.99
_____	29597-7 CARNAL INNOCENCE	$5.50/6.50
_____	29490-3 DIVINE EVIL	$5.99/6.99

Iris Johansen

_____	29871-2 LAST BRIDGE HOME	$4.50/5.50
_____	29604-3 THE GOLDEN BARBARIAN	$4.99/5.99
_____	29244-7 REAP THE WIND	$4.99/5.99
_____	29032-0 STORM WINDS	$4.99/5.99
_____	28855-5 THE WIND DANCER	$4.95/5.95
_____	29968-9 THE TIGER PRINCE	$5.50/6.50
_____	29944-1 THE MAGNIFICENT ROGUE	$5.99/6.99
_____	29945-X BELOVED SCOUNDREL	$5.99/6.99

Ask for these titles at your bookstore or use this page to order.

Please send me the books I have checked above. I am enclosing $ _____ (add $2.50 to cover postage and handling). Send check or money order, no cash or C. O. D.'s please.

Mr./ Ms. _____

Address _____

City/ State/ Zip _____

Send order to: Bantam Books, Dept. FN 16, 2451 S. Wolf Road, Des Plaines, IL 60018

Please allow four to six weeks for delivery.

Prices and availability subject to change without notice.   FN 16 - 4/94